Golden Handcuffs Review

Golden Handcuffs Review Publications

Seattle, Washington

Golden Handcuffs Review
Publications

Editor

Lou Rowan

Contributing Editors

Andrea Augé
Nancy Gaffield
Peter Hughes
Stacey Levine
Rick Moody
Toby Olson
Jerome Rothenberg
Scott Thurston
Carol Watts

LAYOUT MANAGEMENT BY PURE ENERGY PUBLISHING, SEATTLE

PUREENERGYPUB.WORDPRESS.COM

Libraries: *this is Volume II, #30.*

Information about subscriptions, donations, advertising at:
www.goldenhandcuffsreview.com

Or write to: Editor, Golden Handcuffs Review Publications
1825 NE 58th Street, Seattle, WA 98105-2440

Contents

RESPONSE

Late Driver

John Muckle

Pauline didn't learn to drive until relatively late in life. She must've been at least forty-five years old, and the reason for it was her need to drive between the various branches of Antoinette's. Her job there was to organize and supervise the staff, make sure their new lines were being presented properly, were actually selling, and old stock duly palmed off on the matrons. There had been various earlier attempts to motorize her, but neither the early red scooter nor sporadic tuition from Bill behind the wheels of various small cars that had come his way over the years had resulted in anything except a lot of frustration. Either he couldn't teach her or she couldn't learn, not from him. There had been a lot of blow-ups, which always ended in rows and tight-lipped silence or open anger. Bill said she would not be told; she said he couldn't explain himself or let her do anything properly. The only iron she would ever be able to handle was a steam iron.

Bill had taught several other people to drive quite easily, and they had commented on his relaxed, confidence-inspiring manner; but with her, he seemed to lack patience. Once she had even had a few lessons from somebody else; that too had come to nothing – at least not what the offerer of those lessons had wanted – and, finally, when it was really needed, she had learned at a driving school and passed her test without difficulty. It was as though she'd always known how to drive, which is what Bill had always been telling her, so he said, but she wouldn't believe him. All the same, she was reluctant to let him go out with her, except once or twice at the very last minute, to practice before the test.

Her first car had been a mini, her second a VW beetle like Bill's father's, in which she'd felt a bit safer up against the big lorries, and finally an Opel Kadett that had happened to come along. She was driving it right this minute over Marlow bridge, following the morning traffic past the naked lady statue, seated demurely on her plinth and dabbling her teenager's feet in the Thames, turning right through the old pleasure centre of this ancient riverside town towards Antoinette's, which should have been open for an hour by now. She parked on The Causeway, checked her make-up in the rear-view mirror, a touch up on the lipstick, and treated herself to a cigarette: a picture of mature and well-dressed elegance, a model of a customer, in fact, her handbag over her forearm; she pushed in through the dark wooden door and a bell jangled on its bouncy bracket.

The women were huddled in the back of the shop – Mrs. Finch, dowdy, moody Jacqueline, and Ursula, a bony-looking girl of about thirty-five whom Pauline had never really liked. As she approached she noticed that Jacqueline had been crying, dabbing at her eyes with a crumpled handkerchief. It was often this way when she arrived. They seemed to need her to mollify them, set their lives straight. They struck her as naughty schoolgirls, people who couldn't get on with things on their own and were always waiting for her to sort out their problems: minor things which she thought Mrs. Finch should've been able to cope with herself. After all, she was being employed as manageress of the branch.

The trouble was, they didn't like one another very much either. Instead of co-operating and working things out between them, they were always trying to get the best of one another, do one another down. In this case it was a simple matter of arranging the shifts so that Jacqueline, who was having severe problems with her husband and her daughter – it sounded to Pauline like he was a real bully, always throwing his weight around, just the sort of thing she hated – could take Friday afternoon off to go to an event at her daughter's school. She was wOrried about how she was getting on there and she wanted a chance to speak to her teachers properly about some problems she was having. It seemed she'd been accused of something, although the details of exactly what had never come out, and although Pauline could see why the other women got fed up with her moaning, she failed to see why Mrs. Finch couldn't just say yes on this occasion and they would manage somehow, just the two of them. Finally, she said she would come over herself, to which Mrs. Finch said, "Oh, there's really no need."

The clothes, the new lines – dresses, skirts, and tops – were all on their racks. Pauline walked up and down them, straightening the odd ruffled item, smoothing them here and there, while the other women stood back watching her inspection. When she was satisfied that everything was immaculate she quickly chose two items – a pair of wide black silk trousers and a blouse printed with large orange flowers and dark, twisting stems – and asked Ursula to put them on the mannikin nearest the window, replacing the pale green tweed suit it wore currently, or rather, she changed her mind, just move the suited dummy further back to the suit display, and bring out and dress another mannikin from the storeroom. Once she had done that, Pauline herself would accessorize it.

Ursula lifted the dressed mannikin to the back of the shop and parked it in front of the suits rack. She went through to the back and reappeared with another dummy, naked, and older. Its breasts were more prominent, lipstick painted on in fifties style, pursed lips, moulded perm, and thinly plucked eyebrows. Pauline thought of telling her to take it back and get one of the slimmer, blank-faced dummies, but decided that this one would look alright, a change, something a little bit old fashioned, brought back, so said nothing for the time being.

Ursula obviously knew what she was doing. She lifted the

mannikin from its base, upended it expertly and slid on the trousers, which she pinned to prevent them from falling down. She fitted an ample bra and the blouse was soon on over it. Ursula then got to work with a mouthful of pins to try and give some shape to the model and the baggy, flowing garments. She concentrated intensely, absorbed in her work, and by the time Pauline returned with a pair of knee-length stockingettes and a pair of elegant, casual shoes in beige, she was ready to stand back and look at her work. Pauline moved in, and before long the mannikin was looking good, and the presence of two serious women seen through the window had drawn in a few passing customers to look around the shop.

Pauline broke off from her work on the mannikin to ask if she could be of any help to the customers. They were mostly women in their thirties and forties, with a few older ladies. Mrs. Finch and Jacqueline were alert but low key at their stations. It was with the older women that Pauline felt she came into her own. Women in their thirties, she felt. generally knew what they wanted to look like; they had their own sense of style worked out, whereas older women tended to feel they were lagging behind, which they generally were, and needed the advice of somebody closer to their own age, deferential although more glamourous.

Somebody like Pauline, resplendent in her fine ruby red sweater-dress, flaring away from the waist in fine pleats, her volumized chestnut perm, her gold accessories, and her colouring and her delicate, aquiline nose. Pauline knew how to talk to them, how to light a flame in their hearts: she genuinely had the power to make them look better than they ever had before, not to speak of a magical ability to compel self-belief through not so subtle flattery which played on their sense of superiority to others.

Before midday they had between them sold several versions of the ensemble displayed on the mannikin, which was now completely accessorized but in danger of losing her clothes again as the blouses ran low. Even the lime green tweed suit had found a buyer, located beside the rack of suits ably womaned by Mrs. Finch, Jacqueline helping customers in and out of the fitting rooms, Ursula primly but competently handling summer frocks, convinced that it was her pinning which had triggered this particular burst of trade. The spate ebbed at 11.45 am when their class of customer became too frazzled to do anything other than a stop for coffee or lunch, and the women took an opportunity to make a cup of tea and take the weight off their feet on the four old bentwood chairs beside the small storeroom.

Pauline and Ursula smoked. Jacqueline and Mrs. Finch were far happier and more relaxed than they had been earlier, and after a chat and a glance at her slim watch, Pauline said it was time for her to head over to the Walton-on-Thames branch to see how they were getting on with everything. After a few words of advice about the new and old stock – Pauline thought one or two of the summer coats could be brought out and displayed since the weather was so unsettled –she put her own coat on and headed towards her car for the thirty-mile drive to Walton-on- Thames. She bought a cheese salad sandwich on the way and ate it at the wheel, checked her make-up again and carefully inched out into the steady stream of lunchtime traffic where one thing was more or less similar to another.

Bill said this. But then again, he would, wouldn't he? Still, she found that the sense of concentration, of rhythm she had achieved in the shop left her with enough power of self-extension to carry her easily as far as Staines. The familiar if tricky journey unfurled under her wheels through villages and intersections. It was nothing really, as, concentrating intently on the road, she let he mind replay some of the conversations she'd had in the shop that morning. Ursula worked well if she was watched, but that was true of all of them, wasn't it? Mrs. Finch and Jacqueline had resolved their conflict, for now. She felt as though she had bodily lifted them through the morning, and was tired by the effort of filling them with her light; however, she could push this feeling away by moving out into the passing scene, anticipating Walton until the voices of customers and the words she had spoken to them to clinch sales faded out in the wisps of trues and trees and landmark white houses strewn along her route, their rooves glittering with the new solar energy panels: the turnings she'd have liked to live in.

Pauline had been miles away. It wasn't until she was taking the third exit from the Staines roundabout on the A244 that she noticed that the car she drove was no longer an Opel Kadett, it was a navy-blue Volkswagen beetle. Suddenly it was lighter at the front, wider and longer than the Opel, the bonnet sloping downwards, engine droning away behind her, and yet she felt she'd been driving it all along. She had, hadn't she? She glanced in the rear-view mirror, reached, and felt behind her. The summer raincoats she had brought from Cobham that morning to take to Walton were still there in their polythene wrappers. The ashtray was pulled out from the dash and a half-smoked cigarette she remembered lighting was crammed in there, extinguished with her lipstick around the filter.

Somewhat reassured that nothing was amiss, that she was driving along in the perfectly familiar car she normally drove, she turned right. Bill had got rid of the Opel, she remembered, bought her this newer automatic, which she had become so used to that she thought for a moment it was the old green metallic Opel Kadett, a stylish little car she had been able to handle quite comfortably. There was a wide avenue of remembrance leading into the centre of Walton. She found herself on it, looking out for the second roundabout which would take her straight into the shopping centre – so modern and different from Marlow – where she would have to park in the multi-storey and walk down to the shop, which wasn't in the precinct itself but in a road facing it, alongside some other posher premises.

Pauline parked and walked down to the shop, with the coats over her arm. This year's summer stock had been particularly hard to come by, in a way, and the strange event of a couple of months ago had thrown her off balance, but it had also brought out a determination in her, in a way it had confirmed her new power. She had attended a fashion show of one of the big houses in Oxford Street. That day she had been done up to the nines so she could stand up to the other buyers, the women from the big London shops and chain stores. At first, she had thought she would be overwhelmed by it all, but she wasn't, and now she usually looked forward to her buying trips. And it was always very interesting for her to see what they bought, and of course, the reps from the fashion wholesalers were all over you to buy certain things. Pauline knew what she wanted; she just knew what would go with her customers: tasteful, with a bit of dash. She knew the type of colours they liked – russet, with a slash of brightness; and the patterns – bold but not too gaudy. She enjoyed talking to the other buyers, most of them middle-aged women like herself, and the catwalk show itself – well, it was fantastic! Pauline took note of things she liked, marked them in the catalogue, and later placed her orders with one of the assistants.

It had been afterwards on the escalators, down and then up, at Oxford Circus, that she had been in a world of her own, tired, quite hot and a bit stressed, just standing there. Her mind had been elsewhere as she was jostled, as usual, and people had pushed behind her, and looking back on it she felt a shadow, a man she supposed, moving behind her, flickering, the shadow of a man, and thought nothing more about it, this shadow, until she was coming up on another escalator at Waterloo station, and felt a soft breeze on her skin rushing up from the tunnels. She thought of the trains pushing hot air around and it was a pleasant feeling, but then she suddenly thought she shouldn't be feeling it through her clothes.

Emerging onto the busy concourse, she realized that her clothes, including her light summer coat and the dress beneath it, had been cut from behind with a sharp blade, and were loosely flapping apart and away from her body. Her underwear was showing right through. She was indecent. She stood there in the middle of the passing crowds, feeling naked, exposed, but nobody seemed to notice her. She turned right and descended into the Ladies' loos, where she turned her back to the mirror above the sinks and looked over her shoulder. At the back of her clothes was cut to ribbons, hanging off in layers, cut right through to the skin. The knife, or razor, or whatever it was had been pulled right down, so that her backside showed, even the back of her stockings and suspenders, obviously used with considerable force, although her skin itself had not been touched. Everything was completely ruined. She thought of the shadow she had felt moving behind her, that jostle on the Oxford Circus escalator. She had thought nothing at the time., Now she found she was shaking like a leaf, but it only lasted for a few moments. Until she managed to gain possession of herself.

One or two women coming in from upstairs or letting themselves out of the cubicles glanced in her direction, but none of them spoke to her, just passed by, and climbed up to catch their trains. Pauline locked herself in one of the cubicles and took the coat and dress off. She sorted through her handbag and found a few safety pins in the bottom, with which she pinned together the back of her dress and her coat as best she could. It still looked terrible, but there was nothing else for it but to get home somehow, catch her train and get out of this hell hole. On the way, she passed a pair of policemen but she didn't approach them – what could they have done? – and they didn't look at her either. Perhaps they could arrest her for indecency, she didn't know. She looked up at the clacking boards which showed the trains. Fortunately, hers was waiting for her. She got into a smoking carriage and sat in a corner, her bag on her knees, and lit a cigarette with her gold lighter, noticing that her hands were, in fact, still trembling. She managed to get it alight and inhaled deeply. Then she felt a little bit better. She didn't normally smoke on trains. It was unladylike, the sort of thing Joan would have done.

She found her car reassuringly where she had left it in the station carpark, the metallic green Opel Kadett, and drove home, feeling numb inside. Bill was sitting there in the living room with Mikey, waiting for her to get home and cook their dinner. Pauline had gone straight upstairs to change, and it was only when she'd failed to come down after fifteen minutes that Bill came up to see what was wrong. She showed him the clothes and explained what had happened. But Bill had become angry with her, as though it was her fault that she'd been attacked by this maniac, this shadow creature. He asked her to go through it again as if he didn't understand, which she did, and then she started shouting at him. She realized that he didn't believe her.

Pauline pushed in through the door of the Walton-on-Thames branch with the summer coats over her arm, into a situation that was even worse than that she had found in Marlow that morning. The women were just standing around, the place looked chaotic and they hadn't had a single customer. As if they didn't have problems enough, Paul had been in with Nicole and had started shouting at them. Taking her cue from her husband, Nicole, a petite, sharp-featured Frenchwoman, had been sneery and spiteful to Mrs Cassell, the branch manageress, telling her she was an idiot in an all-too-comprehensible accent, and commenting to one of the girls that she looked scruffy and should go home and change into something more appropriate. The girl, Roberta, had left immediately; and was unlikely to return., so said Mrs. Cassell.

In spite of being in an old building the shop was wider and shallower than the other branches, with more window frontage, which might have made for some attractive displays but now only revealed chaos within. Paul's business plan had been to take over existing dress shops that were struggling and turn them around. Walton was an exception to this – it used to be a record shop. Nicole was to have managed them but had little aptitude or patience for the job. She had no idea, really, what this type of English woman wanted to wear, so despite her own stylishness had turned out to be something of a liability. Pauline had been a Godsend to her boss. He asked her advice on everything, paid her well but expected a lot in return.

She was supposed to oversee the refit of the shop, but honestly, the task had been beyond her. Paul had drawn-up plans in the end, and the shopfitters had moved in and spruced up a quick job over one weekend, and the result was that nothing looked right, and the floor space always had a half-unpacked look. It was obvious now that Paul's design had split the shop in half with a till in the middle from which whoever was on it gazed vacantly out at the street beyond. Accessories and tops were on one side and skirts and dresses on the other, which made it awkward to move back and forth, to compare things. The changing rooms were poky and inadequate, storage space poor, and the full-length mirror wouldn't swivel properly and seemed to cut most people off at the neck. It was difficult for customers and staff alike not to feel like spare parts on view to all and sundry, a sideshow for scores of passers-by on a busy corner.

Nevertheless, she had to admire Paul. He was clever. He had good ideas. He did really well with them – he just seemed to know how things worked, more or less. And he did brilliantly, considering he had that Nicole hanging around his neck. She was never satisfied with anything. She made his life a misery. A few weeks ago he'd been considering suicide, walking over Marlow bridge and thinking of throwing himself in the Thames – Nicole had been tormenting him so much, how she was going to leave him and go back to France – but he knew he wouldn't drown and Pauline made him laugh about that on the phone when he called her to share his anguish, and it had been that laughter which had finally got him to hang up and go to bed. Pauline didn't see how long it could go on though, not very long she wouldn't have thought before everything fell apart. He relied on her too much – and didn't seem to understand she had her own life to live, her own problems and difficulties; although while she was talking to him they seemed distant and she would have been hard put to say what they were – if he'd ever shown the faintest interest.

Paul seemed to think she was marvellous: a woman of limitless resources and energy, and often spoke of how much he admired her resilience, thanking her, thanking her again for everything and for listening in detail and for so long to his stories of unhappiness and his difficult relationship with Nicole. Now he had left her to sort out his mess again – offering her only the advice that he had the greatest confidence in her and that she had carte blanche to do whatever she wished with the staff, the shops: everything was in her hands.

Everybody seemed to think a great deal of Pauline. This was something she always had in her favour. Her first action was to ask Mrs. Cassell for Roberta's phone number and to call her up in front of them. "This is Pauline speaking," she said. "You can come back now, she's gone."

And so, Roberta came back and Pauline worked with Mrs. Cassell and her and Florence for the rest of the afternoon. They tidied the shop up a bit, tried out some of the wheeled chrome racks in different positions and dressed a dummy in an outfit from the new stock, with one of the summer coats thrown over its shoulder, a loosely-tied scarf at the neck. All this activity resulted in nothing like the flood of customers in Marlow, but one or two women did come in and look through the racks. and although Pauline knew by instinct about how to leave well alone, when to offer help, this afternoon none of them bought anything. If this went on the shop would have to close and they would all lose their jobs. But why didn't it work in Walton? What was so different about Marlow and Cobham? Pauline didn't know, and she knew from experience that it wasn't going to be worth asking any of this particular bunch of women, who had applied, had been taken on by Paul and Nicole, and had seemed alright at the time. They had no idea at all about anything. Unless it was the shape of the shop itself, the awkward dog-leg of it right on the corner. They were useless really, far worse than the Marlow women, especially Mrs. Cassell and Florence. Pauline had got to know them; she didn't have the heart to tell Paul to get rid of any of them.

Just after four o'clock, a solitary woman of about forty-five came into the shop. She was quite short, a little plump. Something about her bearing, and especially her voice, revealed her as county, and, Pauline thought, a bit stupid. She was the customer from hell but nothing was going to deter her from making sure she bought a complete outfit. The funny thing was it came true again. Somehow – she didn't really know how she did it – she hefted the woman upwards, caught and held her in her eye-beams and by means of her curving mouth, her flaring aquiline nostrils (somebody had once noticed that they always looked as if they had blood in them) and the nuances of her clever, detached voice, soothing, stroking, made her customer laugh with her. She was going to her daughter's wedding or something. After forty minutes the woman left the shop with more bags than she could comfortably carry.

After that ordeal, Pauline needed a cup of tea and a cigarette. She drank it with the others, offering Roberta (the only other smoker) one hanging like a loose tooth from her packet to celebrate their unique sale of the day. It was nearly twenty past five when she left the shop. She was feeling exhausted, her calves ached from so much standing around and she had pain across her back from the anticipated stress of more driving. She would never enjoy it the way men did – for her, it was simply a necessity. On her way back to the multi-storey she popped into a supermarket and bought some things for tonight's dinner. A packet of chicken kievs, a bag of frozen chips, frozen peas (she couldn't remember whether there were enough left in the packet she had used yesterday), and as an afterthought a couple of jars of bloater paste for Bill's future sandwiches, a loaf of bread and a box of Mr Kipling apple pies.

She climbed up to the third floor of the multi-storey – she couldn't be bothered to wait for the stinking lift - and put her shopping in the passenger seat of her little red mini, the car that had served her so well on her many zig-zag journeys back and forth across Berkshire and Surrey, slid into her seat with relief, fastened her seat belt and turned the key. She handed her ticket in to the man at the barrier and the pole swung up and she rolled out into the rush hour traffic of Walton-on-Thames. Although only six miles from home she knew it was going to be a tortuous journey, just when everyone else had been struck by the same idea of getting home quickly. She was already feeling claustrophobic as she thought of edging slowly bumper to bumper back down the Avenue of Remembrance turned into reality. She was, to tell the truth, beginning to find the car cramped and wondered if Bill might be able to find her something a bit roomier. She didn't feel completely safe in the Mini. She never had done. She always felt she might be crushed by a lorry.

Brought to a halt, she reached forward and took the half-smoked cigarette from her ashtray and lit it with the slim Ronson in her hand. This last part of her journey home always wound her up tight. Bill said she should get away earlier, before the rush hour, but she never could. She was always exhausted, her thoughts darting homeward with darker focus, closed down to that end, and all the things she might have said to the women or to Paul or anyone else were directed towards the men at the end of her journey. Sitting there. Waiting for her. These thoughts swarmed up like wasps in her brain, as if a great cloud of the things had got into the car, were attacking her, stinging her as she inched forward in the tiny sweatbox, filling up the space with their dark furry bodies and crawling all over her. It would have been so clever if somebody had known how to kill them all.

But she found her gap and broke right through it in a wave, moving along now in reasonable traffic past the densely-planted woods at the edge of St George's Hill, and felt every summit and plummet on the Seven Hills Road pushing her heart up high as the car hopped over the bumps, and by the time she'd pulled up in front of the house in Lockhart Road, picked up her shopping and walked in through the kitchen door, the wasps were feasting on her body, covering her like a black electrical shroud, so that she was pushing a charged cone of anger sharp end first into the room where they sat waiting for her, innocently watching a VHS cassette of motorcycle racing.

"Are you quite comfortable in there?" Pauline called in a harsh, metallic tone. "Are you feeling quite comfortable?" As she spoke the first of the wasp-squadrons lifted from her shoulders and swarmed in through the gap of the half-open door. The two men sat there murmuring patiently as they waited to be stung, untroubled to be the cause of her nightly blow-up, targets of her controlling rage.

After dinner Bill washed the plates up and made her another cup of tea. Pauline went upstairs to change out of her work clothes, but she found herself too tired to run a bath. Instead, she put her nightdress on and a dressing gown over it, and sat with Bill in front of the television, her feet in a bowl of hot water with a towel under it into which she had sprinkled some red Radox crystals. Mikey had gone upstairs to listen to some music Only the table lamp beside her chair was on, and a standard lamp beside the big old broken-down radiogram, a Grundig that had once belonged to Bill's father. Finally, after all that, she subsided into a truce for the sake of what she really wanted: the peaceful rest of her own inward thoughts. Once this job came to an end, she knew she would never drive again There was a film or a documentary or something on, but she couldn't concentrate on what it was about. Bill watched intently in the shadow-light as the world sped before his eyes.

Pauline lay back on her recliner with her cat. Mr. Jinx, a large, lazy tortoiseshell, was fast asleep on her lap. She was being soothed by the continuous circling vibrations of his flopped out body, heavy and inert, his weight on her abdomen holding her in place, firmly on the ground, her eyes hooded in semi-disgruntled torpor. And not long after he had decided to climb up to bed for the night, Bill hobbled out to the kitchen and pulled down the single grey blind. For a few moments he looked blankly out into the road, where at the kerb, beside the grass verge, stood the pale, gleaming vehicle. The gold-plated Opel. Metallic blue. Metallic light green, or whatever colour it had been originally.

Robin and Jim

Peter Quartermain

Things intensified after the summer of 1948, with Robin and Jim and me facing School Certificate exams at the end of the year, in July. Most kids, they'd be a year or two older than me, 'd be leaving school after that, so would Jim and Robin, but if I passed and did well enough I'd probably do what Our Kid'd done a year ago and move up to the Sixth Form and with luck get into university. Phil'd gone into the Science Sixth but there was no way I wanted to do that, I really hated Science, I didn't like the messy stinks of the Chemistry lab, and when we got to electricity in Physics I got completely lost, it didn't make any sense at all. Water was something I could see, as easily as I could see length or height, but volts and amps were absolutely beyond me. I couldn't for the life of me figure watts out, there was nothing to watch except needles on a meter or filaments in a light bulb, and all the terms in the textbook were defined by other terms I simply didn't get. What good was it to say, "we obtain the number of watts by multiplying volts by amperes" when all it told me about a volt was that it's a "unit of potential" and an ampere a "practical unit of intensity." Utterly meaningless. I knew that if I didn't go into the Arts Sixth I'd go *no*where.

Jim and Robin didn't have that sort of trouble. Robin had

his future mapped out for him on his dad's farm after he got through agriculture college at Sutton Bonington, and so far as I could see Jim wasn't bothered by anything at all, he went off home so many weekends that I began to think of him as a part-time boarder, never free on Saturdays and Sundays. But we still stuck together the way we had before, and we knew that whatever happened we'd still see each other after they'd left school and I'd stayed on, they lived close enough for that.

So far as the three of us were concerned School Certificate really did matter and we had to do well. You wrote not just one exam in one subject but a whole set of them in pretty well everything, it'd take nearly all week, one every morning, one every afternoon, two or three hours at a stretch, no breaks. "What you'll be doing for the rest of your life, and how you'll get on, depends on that exam," Henry Houston more than once told us, "so you'd all better pull your socks up and get on with some work, learn something before it's too late! You can't be just rabbits for your whole life!" *Munch, munch*, I thought, I couldn't help smiling to myself, *Lettuce doesn't grow on trees!* I remembered the eleven-plus exam I'd taken to get properly into Brewood when Broggie came, and I said how easy that'd been. Henry nodded as Prendergast said, "It won't be like that at all, will it Sir. You have to *know* things, how to *do* stuff." "Yes," Henry said, "what we've been doing in Geography. Map-reading, working out from the contour lines what you can see when you look along the coast or through a mountain pass, what's hidden behind a headland. Show you can *use* the map, and that you can *think*." *Like maths*, I thought, *or French. My French is pretty bad.* "You'll have to write an essay in French," King Evans had told us. "You have to take an oral exam if you take the Higher Certificate, and you'll need that if you go to University. You should learn some idioms anyway, it really helps to work those in," but he didn't tell us any. "You have to read some books in French," he said, "like *Eugénie Grandet*, that's the set book in the Sixth Form. Make it sound like a language people *speak*. That always persuades the examiners." Of course King's advice just like Henry's warning fell like water off a duck's back, and I never did get down to reading that set book, not all the way through. Somewhere and somehow I came across a few idioms and got so proud of *fleur à* that in July I actually worked it into a one-page French essay twice, my essay effort concocting some sort of excuse for its generally irrelevant presence and no doubt affording the examiner a moment of exasperated weary humour, but I did manage to scrape through and get the mark I needed. Of course, like pretty much everyone else, I left it all to the last minute. "It's a long way off," Jim said, "plenty of time before the end of the year." He looked round. "Besides, School Certificate won't really make much difference to me," and when I asked, "Oh. I haven't told you yet." We hadn't seen each other all summer, and he said, "After I've done the School Certificate I won't be back." He lowered his voice a bit. "It's not settled yet, but we're probably going overseas, another country." That came as a surprise, we'd no idea. "We're keeping it quiet till it's settled, But Dad thinks he's got a job in Canada. So while we're here I've got to get whatever I can, especially my school certificate." And I could hardly believe my ears. *How could he* do *that? Terrible change, a bit frightening.* "Can't talk about it" Jim said, "not when it's all up in the air. There's a lot we've got to do, just simply so we can go, passports and stuff, lots to think about. It's not like just moving house y'know, the way Filo just did to Lichfield."

He blinked as he said that, took his glasses off and wiped them, and I nodded. But what a shock! All the way to Canada! I didn't know what I thought about that *Where would he be? What sort of place?* My life'd be so strange with Robin gone from School, Jim all those miles away, and me still here in School, in the Sixth Form, all of us in different places, gone for good. I couldn't think what to say. All I knew about Canada was from my stamp collection, with its pictures of pine forests and combine harvesters and fishermen, and it'd been a long time since we'd had to read that Fourth Form book about sod-busting the prairie, I didn't even know if Jim'd be in a town, let alone in a city, and with his usual streak of practicality Robin said, "It must be a worry. I've heard you can't take more than five pounds out of the country. You won't get very far on *that*. Exciting though. Bound to be interesting." And I wondered. I'd heard Dad talk about currency restrictions but had no idea what they might mean to anyone. "How will you manage?" Robin asked, "how can you move to another country if you can't take anything with you?" and Jim said "We'll just have to manage. But dad's looking after all that, says we might be able to get permission to take stuff with us so long as we can't sell it, and he'll have job. Can't take anything valuable with you though, like antiques. You can't even take a stamp collection if it's worth more than five quid," and I thought of his dad's stamp collection, how proud he was of it, much bigger than Jim's, he must've spent years putting it together *How could you get rid of something like that?* "Will he have to sell it?" I asked, and wondered *What's the good of that if you can't take your money?*

"What about Griffiths?" Robin asked. "You should talk to *him*. He lived in Canada all through the War. He could tell you a whole lot," and Jim and I both nodded *Good idea!* We all knew Griffiths of course, how could we not? Griffiths'd turned up in 1946 as a new boy and gone straight into IV A, that made him senior to us, and I'd never even spoken to him he looked so exotic with his self-possessed air and his button-down shirt collars. Dad said Americans "don't even wear proper shirts, don't have our sense of dress at all" and Mum frowned, "Do they use collar-studs? I don't think they even know about detachable collars, I think they just take things to the laundry. So very extravagant." But a week later Jim said he'd learned a lot when they talked, and liked him. "He didn't tell me much really, hadn't lived in a big city like Toronto, made it all sound okay. Said it took him a while to get used to pounds shillings and pence and cars on the wrong side of the road but it's not much different from here. He's a nice guy, he actually listened to what I was saying. I feel a lot better about the move." And then he said, "Remember last year's Sports Day? How he just did it and looked pleased?" and Robin said, "He didn't boast, just did it. Like everything else he does, makes it a matter of course," and who could forget that Sports Day? He looked slow and heavy, this new kid from the Fourth Form, but Barnett on the First Eleven football team said Griffiths was a good middle-distance runner, "slow and steady, great stamina," but what did that mean, sorting runners like that.

We soon discovered that he could really sprint too. Every time his foot came down his head and shoulders slumped forward then straightened up, awful hard work, but he did better than anyone else at the Junior level, came in first or second eight times, from the hundred yards to the mile, sweaty and tired and pleased, just enjoying himself, big smile whether or not he won. We'd laughed in wonder when he won the Cricket Ball Throw, all of us lounging about in the sun, Barker as usual sprawled on the grass surrounded by his pals, a quick flurry and Morgan's indignant "Ow! That really hurt! *Quit* it!" as Barker pulled hard on the seedy grass-stem he'd twisted into Morgan's hair, "You drew blood! For Christ's sake *stop!*" Even Barker perked into attentiveness as Griffiths got to the head of the contestants' queue. None of us ever paid much attention to that event, the contestants standing about so much between throws nothing happening, but one of the kids from Codsall'd said, "You don't want to miss this, it's amazing!" so we eyed the contestants waiting their turn at the canal end of the First Pitch and five or six Masters acting as judges halfway down the field to mark exactly where the ball'd land. Griffiths ran up to the crease-line *Blimey he's fast!* drew back his right arm and unwound, a lovely smooth flow, and *Crikey! Look at that!* some of us speechless as the judges all suddenly scampered and scrambled, Buddha Anderson almost falling over himself to get out of the way as the ball landed and bounced right where they'd all been standing and only Angus stayed put, he didn't even move an inch, he'd kept his artist's eye on the cricket ball up against the sky watched it bounce then strolled over to plant a small white peg where it landed, dusted his hands together smiled his elfin smile and looked satisfied as the other judges sorted themselves out. Henry Houston and Ticker measured it off from the crease, Ticker said something, and Henry shrugged as he wrote it down and smiled his tight little smile.

Griffiths'd thrown the ball miles better than the winner of the Senior throw an hour before, nobody came even close, all of us kids flabbergasted *Nobody'll beat that!* We didn't even bother to watch the next competitor, his throw looked so feeble, but "Don't be so mean-minded!" Henry said. "In any other year that throw would've been good enough to win. Certainly none of you reprobates could do as well." Griffiths'd set a School Record with a throw of seventy-one yards, and he did it again only better a month later, a bit more than seventy-two yards at an "Inter-School Athletic Meeting" with Wolverhampton Grammar School, and we all cackled away as the visitors scattered in a hasty jumble as he threw, we had warned them and they'd not listened, old rivals so much larger, richer and posher than us, and snooty with it.

That cricket ball throw made Griffiths a star. "Just a nine days wonder," he shrugged, "Anyone can learn how to throw." And when Jim went to talk to him about Canada a year later he said "I played Baseball before I came back here, outfield. I wasn't too bad, not as good as most of the team. You have to be able to throw, accurately and fast, and we practiced a lot, we all did. Learned how at school. It's not like cricket, that didn't exist where I was," and when Jim told us all this I thought how Griffiths held his bat up above his shoulder as he danced down the pitch to meet the ball mid-air, clout it. "He's not so hot at bat," Robin said, "he doesn't really direct the ball but just swings, tries to turn every ball into a yorker. He gets caught a lot. Or lbw. A lot of power though, when he connects." Griffiths went his own way even at cricket, and he didn't seem to care what anyone thought. "He's very likeable," Jim said, "If we could see more of him we'd be friends, but he's not a boarder, goes home every day when we don't. *And* he's a Prefect." But I wasn't sure that'd make any difference.

At the beginning of Term Our Kid 'd at last been made a School Prefect, not that that'd make any difference to us, he had his own stuff to do in the Upper Science Sixth, and this Term I was a House-Prefect, as a result I had things to do, sometimes I'd get a bit narked when I had to be on Duty and had something else in mind, "Well, you wanted to be a Prefect" Our Kid said, "You can't complain because you've got things to do. School's not just a holiday, y'know." *Shades of Mrs Bailey!* I thought and wagging my finger chorused with him, "You're not here simply to enjoy yourself!" and laughed. In fact there wasn't any reason to get narked, I wasn't on duty all that much and had plenty of time to go off and enjoy myself, do things with Robin and Jim. We often went down Sandy Lane, perhaps we'd see Mrs Hatfield and who knows, perhaps she'd invite us in, a plump comfortable grey-haired woman quite a bit older than Mum, not a bit like her vinegary and school-teachery assistant Miss Butler, she always found a small treat for anyone on kitchen duty when she was there and she even got Miss Butler trained to reward helpers with "a little something." None of us really knew, and we weren't likely to if we didn't live in the village, it was none of our business anyway, but we'd been told she'd used to be Cook over at Weston Hall for the Earl of Bradford, along with her husband who we thought'd been a gardener or perhaps even a gamekeeper, but he'd died or more likely been killed in the Great War, and nobody ever talked about it. Sometimes we got glimpses of what she could do as a *real* cook. On dishes duty one Saturday I watched her squeeze elegant little peaks of coloured mayonnaise out of a paper bag she'd made into a funnel, to surround a huge salmon decorated with cucumber-slices arranged

like fish scales head to tail just like the pictures in Mum's copy of
Mrs Beeton, and she still had time to find us a small slice of light fruit
cake each. We loved the great big platters of broad beans and bacon
she'd come in specially on her day off to make for Sunday supper
when the beans were in season, we almost fought over that food
as the Prefects carefully dished it out, everyone counted the beans
on his plate, we always wanted more. I still now and again hanker
for that smashing treat, chunks of thick salt bacon, the beans all
glistening with bacon grease, bitter undertones from the beans, salty
slight sweetness from the bacon.

  None of us felt comfortable dropping in unannounced and
uninvited, the second or third cottage down on the right, two-up
two-down, front door straight off the pavement, a stone step straight
into the parlour which opened up into the kitchen, stairs in-between
on the left. On warm days she liked to keep the front door open,
and the back, and you could see right through into the garden, an
intense oblong of light greens and reds and yellows the other end of
the dark indoors, a bit of a plum tree and an apple behind it, a low
brick wall holding the raised garden back from what was immediately
behind the cottage, the vague mass of a house looming up in
creamish stone or plaster, the shadow of its bulk, leaves shifting
and murmuring in the sun, red gingham-check curtains framing
the window's beckoning delicate landscape. Lupines and daisies,
picture-book tidy, the eye drawn past the brass glowing here and
there in the room, a brick path outside the back door, connecting all
the cottages the way ours did at Lichfield, a good place to sit. Back
in the kitchen she had a favourite chair by the big iron range, and
we'd walk past quickly, I'd do a little dip, bob my head down a bit and
over to the right as I rubber-necked, half-hid my face behind the peak
of my School cap. The three of us must have looked terribly furtive
about it all, trying to see if she was there, we didn't dare intrude, but
we'd dawdle a bit, hope she'd see us and perhaps even invite us in,
of course she knew perfectly well what we were up to. One Sunday
the bus from Wolverhampton came in just before we reached the
Square and Mrs Hatfield got off, we nearly didn't recognize her in
her street clothes her hat firmly on her head, she put her basket
down to get at her key, I started to say something I'd no idea what,
some sort of reason for being there I suppose but Jim rescued me,
he said "Hullo, Mrs Hatfield, can we help you with that?" and went

a bit pink, we all did, such a pretty daft question but this glimpse of her having a life outside the School was a bit disconcerting, Cook in an old comfortable-looking tweed coat just like Mum's instead of the white coverall she always wore in the kitchen, it looked like Mr Hutchings's lab coat only it was clean. "That's all right, boys, I'm used to managing" she blinked as she smiled, us bursting with curiosity, picked up her basket and said "Do you want to see?" her glasses blinking in the light, "Come on in, then," and we went in and she showed us the parlour, "I like to sit just there," she said, "That's my sister's chair, we make ourselves comfortable" and as we turned to leave she said "It was nice of you to stop just now" and she smiled again. "Perhaps one of these days you'll come by and stop for a visit" and I nodded, I expect the others did too as we said thank you but I felt like a great clumsy lummox, all of us galumphing in on her private life like that.

      We didn't really tell anyone what'd happened. I sort of wanted to boast, knowing Cook in a way the others didn't, but it was too private for that, knowing we could go back. It was our secret, and it was also hers. Talking about it would've been a bit like talking about life at home, personal stuff, nobody else's business. Yet what difference would it make to anybody else if we now and again went to see Cook and she'd fed us tea. I worried that we might be a nuisance and Robin and Jim, once he was coming back again almost every weekend, agreed. "Yes, we've got to be careful not to, but she can always just say Hullo and leave it at that, can't she," and it wasn't long before the three of us got into the hopeful ritual of cutting our Sunday walks a bit short, loop back around the village so we could come up past her house and hope she'd notice. We could always say we'd been down to the village cricket ground across from Dolly Asprey's, we all went quite often down to Deansfield to watch anyway, lots of kids did. Then one Sunday on our way back to School Mrs Hatfield's door was open and Jim knocked hard, stuck his head a bit round the jamb and leaned, "Hullo Mrs Hatfield, we're on our way back from the cricket. It's over already, and we thought we'd just say hullo as we came by. The village won by seven wickets," as if we had anything to do with *that*, and I could hardly believe my ears *How'd he dare do* that? Mrs Hatfield came in from the garden and said "Oh hello boys, I thought I'd heard you. That's nice of you to drop by, would you like to come in for a bit? I haven't seen much of you lately, not even at School. I suppose we've all been busy." She looked back into the garden. "I'm just making myself a cup of tea, and I'm sure you'd like some too. Come in and make yourselves comfortable."

We looked at each other, "I don't –" I started in a low voice. Robin gave me a look and asked "Can we do anything to help?" and she said we could set the table, told us where to find things, and we Nosey Parkered our way around the room, "That's alright," she said, "but don't touch anything!", old photos on the wall, a calendar, a sampler, different kinds of embroidery stitches in all sorts of colours, a lot of them faded, the alphabet, and flowers, and a name and a date, eighteen-eighty-something-or-other, it was too far away to see clearly up on the wall above the mantelpiece and as she came in with a tray she said "I did that when I was a young girl, we all did one in those days. Careful work." I thought of the one at Alcester and told her my Aunt Dot had one on the farm done by her mother a long time ago. Jim said he'd never seen one before and Robin said in surprise "I thought everyone had one" and then nobody said anything for a while. Jim picked something up on the mantelpiece and showed it to Robin and I looked at some of the photographs on the wall as we all fell silent, I couldn't think of anything to say, Mrs Hatfield busy behind me, and suddenly "Why don't you come and sit down?" Bread and butter, little rock-cakes, a bowl of watercress, celery sticks, and she looked at the whatsit Robin and Jim had got from the mantelpiece and said "The Earl of Bradford gave me that, a long time ago, when I'd been working for him for ten years, it's very old brass, it's fragile so be careful, it came from India." I sat on the edge of my chair and looked at the other two, perched on the edge of theirs, "Who are all those photographs?" I asked as Jim pointed "Are those horse brasses? I've seen some of them in shops, but mum and dad aren't interested." "Those are real ones," she said, "they're not fake. They come from the tack room at Weston Park, some from canal horses from before the First War," I thought they were smashing, probably worth a bit, but they weren't, not then, people were just beginning to collect things like that. Dad'd said that the gin palace over in Sutton Coldfield on the main road was full of them, trumpery Brummagem-ware, fake like the beams and the half-timbered outside walls, but I wondered how you could tell. "These are heavy," Robin said, "not flimsy. *Look* at 'em, they're not *machine-*

made." Mrs Hatfield nodded, "the irregularities," she said, and told us the photographs were old too. "People in the village," she said, a big square man with big black muttonchop whiskers his head full of hair, wearing a leather apron, his elbow on the table at his left, his eyes looking a bit astonished over your left shoulder as you looked at him, a slightly cross and bewildered look on his face, full of contained and impatient energy. "He was the village blacksmith," she said, "he died when I was about eight or so, quite an old man by then," it must have been an old photograph then, "Oh yes it is," she said, and pointed to a sepia photo of a great big windmill, great holes in the walls and one of the vanes fallen off, *where's that? There aren't any windmills round Brewood* "There used to be lots," she said, "A big one at Wheaton Aston," and she told us about the metal works and charcoal burners in Penkridge and the maltings and forges at Brewood in the old days, we didn't even know the Spinney'd been dug out by navvies to build the canal embankments. We'd never heard of any of it. We sat there guzzling our watercress sandwiches and celery, and bread and butter and rock cakes. "Didn't anyone tell you about Ironbridge?" We all shook our heads, we'd all heard of it and Robin'd been there once, "Used to be an ironworks there," he said. "I'm surprised you don't know," she said, "It's less than twenty miles away. Where they built the very first cast-iron bridge in the world, two hundred years ago, it's famous, one of the Seven Wonders. A lot of things have happened round here, don't they tell you any of this at school?" She shook her head a bit and told us that Thomas Telford'd built the aqueduct to carry the canal over the Watling Street, we knew the Watling Street of course built by the Romans, we knew that the way we knew Julius Caesar'd invaded England in 55 B.C. "It's made of iron that aqueduct, and Telford's still a famous man," and we nodded. Nowadays a plaque on it says the aqueduct was built in 1832, but there never used to be any notice boards telling people what things were or who they belonged to or where footpaths went, at least not since they'd all been taken down in the War. Nobody'd ever said a word to us about Ironbridge. Perhaps they didn't know, like that teacher who hadn't known how to spell Cheslyn Hay. "Were there iron works round here?" I blurted, and Jim looked at me "Well of course there were, you chump, we're right on the edge of the black country, coal and iron." "There used to be lots of ironworks, but not like Dudley or Walsall" Mrs Hatfield said, "and that's what keeps us all going isn't it, not kings and queens." She looked away. "The Earl of Bradford's a nice man. I liked working at Weston Park. I like going back to visit now and again, but not very convenient from here. You could go over on your bikes."

"I really learned a lot" I said as we three walked back to School. "She knows so much about this place," Robin said, "Who's done what and where. Not what we get in History." "Yeah," I said, "I can never sort out the two William Pitts, What difference do they make, anyway?" and Jim told me not to be so daft, "of course they matter, the way Gladstone and Disraeli matter, it's what they did then that makes us what we are now," but I couldn't see that. It wasn't like Turnip Townsend, he changed the way we grow food, changed farming practice.

We never said a word about our visit to Cook's, but something got about anyway and later that week Buddha said in class "Yes, you know nothing about local history, and you should. The best place to start would be the history of the School, it's been here a long time, four hundred years, just about," and next day he told us about famous people who'd been at the School, we'd never heard of any of them. After less than five minutes on William Pitt, he spent the whole class on Richard Hurd, son of a Penkridge farmer and "our most famous Old Boy," Bishop of Lichfield and then Bishop of Worcester until he died in 1808. "I'm going to set up a Debating Society in the School," he told us, "we'll call it the Hurd Society after him. We ought to have his works in the school library, I'll have to see what we can do about that." We knew no more about Hurd than we knew about William Huskisson, but we delighted in the fact when he told us that Huskisson was the first person in the world to've been killed by getting run over by a train. I told myself "*getting* run over" made it sound like Huskisson did it on purpose, and it was icing on the cake when Buddha said Huskisson'd got run over in 1830 by George Stephenson's *Rocket*, the most famous train of all. But Jim was scornful. "That's not *History*," he said that night, "It's just *gossip*, it doesn't say anything about why people do what they do, it doesn't tell us a thing about how they lived," and I wondered. *Why wasn't talk about the* ancien regime *or the two Pitts just Gossip?* The unbidden memory popped into my head how when I'd been taking Agriculture a couple of years ago because I thought I wanted to be farmer Uncle Tom'd gestured at the field over the hedge. "Take a look at those oats. What d'you think?" I looked at Dad and didn't say anything, that was his and Dad's business, not mine. "No, Peter, I'm asking *you*" Tom said. "You say you want to be a farmer." *What am I supposed to say?* I hadn't even been sure they were oats until he said so, and he said "Look at the leaves, they're a touch yellowy aren't they." And I looked. "Oh," I said, "Yes!" and they were, not that lovely fresh green you get in a young plant. "Need a top-dressing of lime, don't you think?" Dad said, and Tom nodded, "A bit acid, yes." That completely flummoxed me, it wasn't the sort of thing we did at School, we didn't talk about soil conditions, we talked about crop rotation, cattle disease, different sorts of blight, and took dictated notes, but we didn't really *look* at anything. We did drawings and tables for prep, and that wasn't gossip, it was *useful* even if we couldn't actually use it.

But why had we spent so much of last Term learning about bees when there wasn't a single hive anywhere on the school grounds? At Alcester Tom'd walk down to the fields in the summer and pluck an ear of wheat oats or barley and rub it in his hands and blow off the chaff and even bite the grain left in his hand. "What do you think?" he'd ask whoever was with him, "Not quite ready yet, is it," and he'd cock an eye at the weather, so crucial as harvest-time got closer. At School we never got anything about that any more than we got told about John Bright or the Middle Passage. William Wilberforce, yes, he was a hero, but we got nothing about the everyday, what a poet called the attractions of living recorded, just famous names and famous events, powers and agreements, wars and battles, a long way from anything local or even useful. We had to get what Buddha called a "decent grounding," that's what the School Certificate was all about, so we read about Mazarin, Metternich, and Richelieu, and I was completely lost when Buddha told us to write an essay deciding *Was Louis XIV a good king or not.* How would I know? I got an inkling of what I might say when I was complaining about it to Mike Mortimore in Mrs Roberts's tuck shop, he was nuts about history and after doing his national service a couple of years down the road he went to Oxford and got a degree in it, and a kid from the Nash waiting for a bottle of pop looked at Mike and me, "If you're askin' *me*," he laughed, "and yeah I know you're *not*, what do we 'ave kings *for*? What good are *they*?" Coming the way it did, from a Nash kid, that took me by surprise, it was the sort of question a teacher or someone in the Sixth Form might ask, but as we walked out the door Mike nudged me "His dad probably votes Labour" he smirked, and I shrugged. I hadn't connected what we did at School with politics. It wasn't until a couple of years later and I'd left School altogether that I realized I didn't have to be a staunch Conservative like Mum and Dad but could go my own way. Not that I knew what the choices were, *Labour* and *Conservative* were just empty words.

By the time the weather got better and the days longer Jim once again started going home for the weekend more and more. "A lot to do before we emigrate" he said, and I liked the way that word marked him off from the ordinary, "All the kerfuffle and the interruptions get in the way, take up all the time. I never get my prep done," and one Saturday with Robin and me a bit bored and Jim off at home again for the weekend Robin said, "Let's go for a bike ride?" and I gave him a look *Where?* "I don't mean *now*," he said, "but tonight, I mean *really* tonight, after everyone's gone to bed," and that was so outlandish it took me aback. "Colin James does that, quite a bit, him and a couple of others, he says it's terrific, nobody else about, it's ever so quiet, they get everywhere. 'Course, he does it at home, still has to sneak out, but we could do it here. Probably easier. Just have to be quiet." Colin lived close to Wheaton Aston. "Out to the rezzer, over to Weston under Lizard, all over the place, they cover a lot of ground." Suppressed excitement as I lay in bed that night, I didn't have a watch but Robin had his, *Have to get dressed, carry my shoes downstairs, have to be absolutely quiet* and then a quiet shuffling, Robin nudged me, hardly breathing nodding his *come on!* Scarcely a cloud on this clear night, half moon, black shadows, *Watch out! That creaks! Catch the door before it slams!* Colours all washed out, faint clatter as we got our bikes out of the bike shed but no, no sign of anybody. Climb on, a huge sigh of relief, the faint bubble of a laugh wells up, a stifled *whoop* as we pedal through the Gate *Ssssh!* and down School Road to turn past Mrs Roberts's to Church Road and another *Ssssh!* but this time with a grin as we scoot past Newport Street and turn along Bargate from the empty square, faint light behind a curtain upstairs at the Lion, faint *click, click* I can hardly hear but regular as my pedaling foot and breath, a constant register each time the rising crank arm grazed the back strut *click!* pause, and *click!* slight wobble of the pedal *I never did get that fixed!* the quiet susurrus of our tires on the blacktop down Kiddemore Green Road, pale grass, long shadows, stir of movement in the hedge, the sudden loom of something big, heart jump as a cow shifts in the field, a pair of bright eyes and a shadow in the field as you pass by everything quiet except your breath and the tyres, magical, and *Oh!* Robin freewheels almost to a stop, stands in his saddle, points, our bikes quietly ticking as we coast neither of us pedaling *Is that a fox?* the faint hiss of our tires scarcely a disturbance in this transformed landscape, ribbon of road pale under the moon, an owl, the sound of a distant car, flurry of wings dark shadow overhead *that owl! Hunting*, crossing the field from wood to coppice, and you stand on the pedals again to see and the edge of your shirt lifts as you crest a slope, a sudden cool breath of night air at your waist and here's a five-barred gate, soft rustles in the hedgerow *something bigger, that's no rabbit!* Way over the soft patchwork of fields and barns and houses a subdued bark, dog to fellow dog, one farm to another, *relax! it's not us it's after!* a grey and black patched hump across the field melts into a Friesian cow, and then more cows *Whose dairy farm?* A yellow glow outlines the slope ahead of us, trees on both sides, and we scramble off our bikes pull them onto the verge and lay them down *Hurry before it gets here* the doubled V stares into the sky not in a rush but not slow either down the middle of the road, a patch of nettles black behind the stark then washed-out green, yellow carlight defines a shifting patch of weirdly strange yet familiar roadside, and you crouch down to hide your face, you snatch a quick look and blink away the abrupt dazzle and the tears it brought, the light fades round a corner and the engine-sound five seconds after, silence restored. The village doctor on his way back home *who's he been to, this hour of night? Hope it's no one we know* and you resist its faint hint of inside knowledge, possible gossip, climb back on your bike the saddle cool the crossbar cold against your leg the handlebar wet with dew from the long grass you just now put it down in. "Perhaps we should go back" I breathe, "turn round" but we pedal on, down a dip and up the other side *How far is it to the rezzer?* the quiet exhilaration of this silent world as we glide between hedgerows. A light comes on as we cruise past a barnyard *Crikey! What time is it?* We zoom past Butler's farm at the head of Shutt Green Lane but no, we won't get to the rezzer not this trip, save it for the next, silhouettes of trees, the dense ribbon of the Milky Way still dusted across the sky the North Star bright, no faint light of dawn over in the east *It's long before false dawn, the birds are all dead quiet* and we stop to catch our breath and listen. Then we turn back, sneak up the stairs "Gosh, that was smashing! Do it again," get back to bed its sheets suddenly cool against my busy skin, nobody stirs, and I settle.

But "*I don't know,*" Jim said next day when we told him about it at Break, what we'd done and where we'd been, "It sounds terrific. Yes, I'd like to do that, sounds fun." He looked at me. "But I'm not so sure. We're all senior, 'n' Peter *you're* a Prefect. What'd you do if you caught someone from the first or second dorm, junior kids Third Formers doing that, sneaking off in the middle of the night to go for a bike ride, would you let them? Not *do* anything?" None of *them would*, I thought, not *them!* But then *What about seniors?* I thought, and "Well," I said, "Dicky Feltham went off to the rezzer a couple of weeks ago, three of 'em, for a swim in the middle of the night. Been more than once, a lot of people know about that. And they're all in the Sixth Form, they're senior to us. One of *them*'s a Prefect." I remembered what Dad'd called the perks of his job, how scrupulous he was about them. A couple of years back, he'd brought a tin of peaches from the store so we could have a treat, "We only got one case, twenty-four large tins, for the whole store, sold them all as we were putting them on the counter. Ridiculous, really," he'd said to Mum as he handed it over, "I've already paid for it, and taken the points from my ration-book." I didn't say anything about that to Jim but it's what I had in mind. You have to *earn* the privileges of rank, I thought, that's why they're called *privileges*. But Jim shook his head, "That's not honest. we all have the same *rules*. And it's not *fair*. You can't go bogging off to enjoy yourself when you've told everyone else they can't, that's hypocritical. Rules should be the same for everyone," and settling down to sleep that night I feared Jim was probably right.

As it turned out we only went off at night a couple of times after that, perhaps there was a connection. "Nothing to stop you doing it at home" Jim said, "but you'd have to tell your mum and dad what you're doing. Where you're going, too. Something could happen." As soon as I got home for the summer Mum said "*No!* It's far too dangerous, cycling all those main roads in the dark, no.

Even if you've got good lights on your bike. *No.*" And "besides," Our Kid said, "who'd you go with? It's not a good idea, you can't go by yourself. And cycling in the dark even with a light, specially round here? That's completely *daft*, you'd get run over in less than'n hour!" A month or two later, almost as soon as he left school, once he'd got a job in Birmingham and was living in digs he began to bike home every weekend, Birmingham to Lichfield and back, "I'm used to traffic," he said. "You're not. And I know the back roads," I was glad it wasn't me trying that, though when I got to Nottingham three years later I cycled the three or four miles to school and back every day and it was safe enough. Everyone used bikes.

================

[This is taken from the revised version of Chapter 31 of *Growing Dumb*]

"Thinking the Poem; Thinking the Poem Writing":
An Interview with Rachel Blau DuPlessis

Andrew Mossin

Since completion of her decades-long project in serial poetry, *Drafts* (1986-2012), Rachel Blau DuPlessis has continued her work in the long poem through several book-length poetry projects that includes *Interstices* (2014), *Graphic Novella* (2015), *Days and Works* (2017), *Numbers* (2018), *Around the Day in 80 Worlds* (2018) and *Late Work* (2020), from the series *Traces, with Days*. Her full career as a poet-critic includes a number of books on gender and poetics, including the trilogy *The Pink Guitar, Blue Studios,* and *Purple Passages.* She has co-edited several anthologies and edited *The Selected Letters of George Oppen.*

Continuing her explorations of the formal possibilities of the book as an object of cultural marking and making, DuPlessis has sought in her recent works in poetry to further explore the connections between the visual plane of the page, the poem as documentation of thought, and collage as a visual medium in dialogue with and in movement alongside the poems. The work's ethical edge comes from DuPlessis's continued emphasis on what she refers to here as the "perpetual sense of the between, often between fixed doctrines." As such, DuPlessis's most recent work takes the project of *Drafts* to its next logical stage: further pondering the possibilities of innovative poetries in a time of radical cultural and political upheaval and, in doing so, reframing the usefulness and significance of poetry as both cultural critique and salient documentation of human experience.

This interview was conducted via email between February and May of 2020.

ANDREW MOSSIN: [AM:] In "Statement on Poetics" included in *Inciting Poetics: Thinking and Writing Poetry*, the recently published volume of essays edited by Jeanne Heuving and Tyrone Williams, you write with regard to the stakes of poetry that "one wants a truth but not the law" (34). This seems like a premier statement of both practice and stance in the work, one that pushes against doctrinaire or camp-based positions while at the same time asserting the importance of ethical responsibility for the work that any poet produces. Has your sense of poetry's ethical charge, its responsibility to claim a position of truthfulness in the culture-at-large, changed over the years? And how?

RACHEL BLAU DuPLESSIS [RBD]: this question has a one-word answer—which is maybe the funniest thing ever to be said in an interview. The answer is "no." It has not changed. Ethical responsibility in language, to language and form are central to the beauties, necessities and longings I want satisfied by poetry.

Two avenues from that fond terseness. One is to allude to more of the argument I made in the essay "Statement on Poetics" that got to the "pull quote" that you have chosen, because it is more intricate than the summary (and perhaps too Law-like!) a citation. Maybe we will need to do this a little. I am keen to say how the "intricate bottomless tangibility" of language in poetry means acknowledging the play of language to evoke, simultaneously, thought, feeling and a formal pulsation in time. I feel poetry is an amazing experience of an intellectual-emotional "between" and an intersubjective between—linking language richness and socio-cosmological scope through you, a reader—this clarity of meaning within richness IS its ethics. And the second avenue, in my response here, is to just give a backstory to pick out some key moments of the path I took in poetry to tell you how my work developed and why you chose this statement as an opening.

I suppose I have commitments but not doctrines. I've been associated and self-associate with only two groups, both of them fluid and not really groupy-groups in my affiliation and experience of them. Over the years I've tried to deepen and further interpret what these two commitments mean and meant, and how my work in poetry (and in poetics/literary criticism) engage with this deepening.

One commitment was to feminist thinking AS a mode of thought— thinking about gender, particularly the roles of gender in culture. Here I was supported both from a general women's movement upsurge, including my ability to teach kinds of women's studies courses, and my connection with the *HOW(ever)* formation, even though I lived far from the Bay Area. The other commitment was to the situational and self-critical thinking of the objectivist position in poetry, as laced with a general saturation in related projectivist formations. Here I was particularly affected by George Oppen's work, especially by doing pioneering scholarship by editing the *Selected Letters*—a document in poetics as well as poetry. I was lucky enough to know both Mary and George Oppen as friends (a friendship that continues with Linda Oppen), but he is not the only objectivist whose work I have studied, since I have written on both Niedecker and Zukofsky.

Thinking with the poem, thinking the poem writing—the goal of both the objectivist and projectivist positions, and where they fuse—can emphatically include thinking about some things some of those writers didn't particularly think about, and involve coming to different conclusions than some of them did. No? Seems logical unless you want "thinking" in poetry always to be self-confirming, at which point it is not thinking at all. This (with a different origin) parallels what Alice Notley says in "Thinking and Poetry," an essay in *Coming After*, an essay containing a wish for maintaining "honest thinking" (158), "ruthlessly honest" seeking "truth as the present reality of this world." This, interestingly, involves starting over and over ("beginning again and again" as a formal stance) to try to see and interpret— something that I find quite idiomatic to my practice. It also involved standing in an odd zone—"too objectivist for the feminists and too feminist for the objectivists." I said this presciently in *The Pink Guitar*, and it remained true for many years.

And "feminism" as a social-historical movement (with many cultural implications) has where necessary tried to change laws and practices toward a greater social justice for women and other groups that experience capricious, ideology-driven, unstable even cruelly delimited senses of social and aesthetic citizenship (applying to other minoritized groups as well). Equality, mutuality of recognitions, and appropriate agency? Who resists this??

Feminism also values various attempts at the representation of women in art and art products and recognizes women (and others) among honorable and serious historical producers of art, poetry, music and so on. Social contributions of many groups to general culture—understood and examined—that's what we want, right? Not self-confirming, self-conforming canons.

The word "feminist" scares people. Who cares anymore? I still remember when Ron Silliman had a blog with reader comments (a brave openness), and in around 2006 he talked about *Blue Studios* positively—it's a book that has some serious gender analyses of poetry in it. The result was a deluge of negative remarks—the most uninformed being how I must be a terrible teacher of men. Huh! As if this person had ever seen me teach! And you, as a former student, testified that this was not true (for which I was and am grateful); you also had a generous statement on me as a teacher in your April 2007 review of *Blue Studios* in *Jacket* 32 [http://jacketmagazine. com/32/mossin-duplessis.shtml] This blog-land event, which was unexpectedly weird, opened a little corner of male partiality and rage to me that now feels like a salvo of other expressions of that rage that have continued—and increased over the next decade. It is the policing of valid analysis—and precisely why I don't like pre-judged and already determined assumption-packs to be the default positions allowed for understanding.

Of course, feminism has gone through changes, and holds many historical positions within it, some unpalatable, unhelpful, and doctrinaire, some themselves racist and sexist and intolerant. I try to evaluate what I do under that rubric which modulated for me into my actual field of study—looking at poetry and poetics through a gender-lens that is not exclusive, but curious and inclusive. And this "call" has led to my gender-inflected critical and essay-inflected work. So in criticism and poetics, I've done a certain amount of serious scholarly, analytic and even influential work. Believe me, I have no apologies, despite some people's uncomfortableness with my analyses of Stevens and race, for instance, or Pound and the intricacies (note that word) of appropriation, or the representation and stakes of male bonding in recent poetic movements.

In poetry, I am bi-lateral, a woman writer in my time and a writer in my time—and those aren't my only functional subjectivities, either. This both/both position (to use Anne Waldman's phrase), has allowed me to do the work I was called to do. This would be—say, early works of mythopoesis (now recapped in a sonnet-essay sequence [as yet unpublished] called *Eurydics*), to works "rewriting" literary history in order to insert some imagined missing women poets (in *Tabula Rosa*), to attempts to stay alert to early motherhood ("Writing" in *Tabula Rosa*), and many, many allusions and stances in *Drafts*, a long poem in 114 cantos from 1986-2012, and in the work I am doing in *Traces, with Days*, a long poem in episodes. Within the next two years, a selection of this work will appear in a selected poems.

On the "objectivist" side of things (insofar as I can separate them), the crucial sense that a poem should be a necessary object, not written for inauthentic reasons (to self-deceive, to "be a poet" since you are supposed to be, to impress, to hold a position telling others what to think). A poem must have necessity—then it has the drive to perfect itself in "intricate bottomless tangibility."

A self-judging existentialism infused Oppen's writing position (against the inauthentic choice) and belatedly rubbed off on me. For a while that led to a self-blocking ultra-seriousness, but I got over it (sez I!) in favor of some fluidity, some wit and musicality, and an architectonic sense of propulsion (as in *Drafts*).

When I had, recently, to write something about my work for the release of *Late Work* by John Yau's Black Square Editions, I realized something like this: I am interested in the nuances of Being (personal and social) in a damaged wondrous world: "the stain of one small life/ among the elements" (*LW*, 83 from "Mackle, Shard and Trace"). I have aesthetic, political-historical, and cosmological interests in my poetry and I don't separate these.

In poetry, one wants to make statements in language in all the social-sensuous means and hyper-saturated nuances that can be mustered toward pleasure and a reverberating impact from formal, tonal and syntactic understandings. Real rhetorical pulse of sheer poesis, not "rhetoric" in the limited sense of straining or poseur manipulations, not in one "position" only. I think that has led me away from "period style." The only "position" I might hold in poetry is the tertium quid—a perpetual sense of the between, often between fixed doctrines. I sometimes think I want more from poetry than most poetry has been designed to give.

AM: *Graphic Novella*, at least according to the publication information I have available, is the second of two new works to be published in English following completion of your long poem, *Drafts* (1986-2012). The first of these, *Interstices*, appeared in 2014, followed by *Graphic Novella* in 2015. The latter is a remarkable assemblage of diverse materials, including meta-commentary on poetry and poetic practice, photographs that are often embedded with your own handwritten notes, newspaper clippings and other media, and a range of diverse materials that altogether narrativize (to use Hayden White's term) the experiences of reading and writing. I wonder if you could reflect on how this book began to take shape and solidified into this form and its place in your career as different from yet an extension of the work you accomplished in *Drafts*.

RBD: Answering this means a little foray into an uncomfortable place—the space between closing up *Drafts* in 2012 and the spaces of a variety of quite different work. After *Drafts*, I felt I had to experiment with changes (no matter what happened). A friend pointed out (in a great Worry) that I was retiring (2011), then (2012) stopping the long poem I'd been composing for 25 years—wasn't I a little afraid of what would happen (that is, in my translation of this message—are you crazy?). The answer was, "yes, a little," and I did not know what would happen (or whether I would regret this risk), but really did cast myself off into projects "experimentally"—to see what would happen. One thing that had begun to occur at the end of writing *Drafts* was writing somewhat shorter poems. Another thing was entering the actual visual spaces of collage, as if instantiating my collage poetics by making visual text as well as poetic structures.

I had begun to make collage again (after a hiatus) first with little vis-po glyphs in around 2002, and then more full scale collages in around 2007. I was trying to attend to a mode of visual art to which I had always been deeply attracted, despite having no particular visual or technical training. I had taken a step into two collage poems in *Drafts* made in color (with text), and only published *in full* in a separate book (a bit rare but in print) called *The Collage Poems of Drafts* (2011). Only excerpts of these works could be published in the black and white format of poetry books—so that is what they are in the last two books of *Drafts*. I was ready for a large serial project mingling writing and collage. I think of the process as "making pages," a rubric whose meanings and scope I am just beginning to understand.

During this period, beginning in about 2012, the political feeling in the US started darkening and getting weirder in ways I had few insights to state in analytic terms. The economic crises, the blockages, and mean-nesses—I just began working intuitively with these political feelings and odd "normal" images in fairly ugly, angry, baffled, and off-putting ways. I literally didn't know what I was doing with collages of Big Cars and Big Cameras and aphorisms. Further, I wanted to make this work in black and white—in part because I assumed (with some naivete) that B&W materials are easier to reproduce and distribute. Color, which I love and love to work with, seemed impractical for this dark, annoyed feeling and for the sources I was using. The work, filled with unease of theme and statement, and unease about what I was actually making, slowly coagulated, image with writing, and got sequenced, thus took shape almost like a "trash book" or "scrapbook," a "summary account involving daily life," at any rate something graphic, flat out about lives today, particularly about "waste people."

Graphic Novella (2015), is a visual-text work of loosely political meditations in prose poems, essay-responses and poems intersecting with and matched with black and white collage. The premise was I have had enough of claims of "the new": being extra-original, working within the aesthetic bounds of "art" to claim to be making newer new and even newer objects as if in a cold war of ratcheting up newness points. I thought "let's just examine 'the news,'" for *it* is dramatic and compelling enough, has deeply disturbing clues and oddly unfitting-together symptoms and disconcerting events and insights. The book thus tries to pass beyond the avant-garde question about what the "new" is in favor of the much more desperate question "what is the news" and how to understand what is going on in every crisis-laden aspect of life: political, economic, ecological, from prison visits to high end luxury goods of cars, watches and cameras, to wars and rips in the fabric of lives, to daily life and ethics. In this work are recurrent visual motifs of the camera, the lens, the watch, legs in an attempt to get into basic aesthetic-ethical observations. I was using these strange combination of items (that I joined intuitively) to constitute a page to "read"—that is to stare at for messages, and to interpret.

This work, constructed and written from about 2012- 2014, is a full-length book of 119 pages in black and white collages, visual combinations, essay commentary, news reports—soundings in the rapidly strange and estranging politics clearer and clearer by 2014, when the title occurred to galvanize this "mess," to 2015, when it was completed and put into print, with a big "CAUT" punning on one side and "CAUTION" on the other side of a cover (designed by me) covered with over-layered news clippings.

With *Graphic Novella*, I had gotten a title in my head (this is often the case with my practice) and had to make a work with that rubric, although I was well aware of the loose ends of its pun. This was not a graphic novel (a work using cartoon and comic book conventions). It was not a novella, either—at least not one with a single plot. "Novella," was a pun on the "new" (on the "nouvelles" as news, and then on the multiply plotted a kind of tele-"novella" going on and on), to end up with a diagnostic book. Also it involved a graphic "confrontative" sense of what one sees in the news That drew on the meaning of "graphic"—depicting something in an overly clear way, too vivid or direct, and maybe embarrassing or distasteful. Thus the work is loosely investigative, with detection and the detective novel being alluded to at a few points. How to represent what is happening "these days." I point out simply that the work was conceived and executed before any of the malfeasance and disasters of the Trump presidency and the complicity of one political party had yet occurred. If this work is about salvage, it's a salvage done to collect and identify clues to the disaster. The work comes to at least one conclusion among others: the whole country—the US—(even a good deal of the world) is suffering from PTSD (post-traumatic stress disorder). Why—first thoughts, endless war, real ecological disaster pending, as with water, precarity, gulfs between the few wealthy and the many. As I write this response in April 2020, we are now inside of the COVID pandemic. A feature of the politics of this book would be noting that many people depicted or evoked in it are treated as detritus or waste—something strikingly unethical. (A good descriptive neologism here before I erased it—depicted/despicted.) They are also "managed people" often—prisoners, their families, mentally-ill woman (with her ranting-writing directly cited), soldiers and vets often damaged, the surveilled (i.e. everyone), the forcibly relocated, women against second class treatment, over-worked workers, those not at the "table" when ecological disaster is being discussed (and when often there is a postponement of any real conclusions or ameliorations of that disaster).

I am extraordinarily lucky that this work was published rather quickly in 2015 (soon after being completed) by mIEKAL aND and Xexoxial Editions. His version had the right degree of "unsleek" finish, and he also put my collage, constructed exactly for this book, on the cover.

It became clearer that doing collage with writing—making that kind of object—a work of collage-poems as a book—does break the frame of the book, particularly a book of (normal) poems. There is some ethos of illuminated manuscript and beauty, the dialogue between image and text, but collage poem work is not afraid of its oddity and potential ugliness. Sometimes the visual texts are illustrative (of the writing it joins), but sometimes these are two different products (visual text, verbal text) that become one. The two respond to each other, gloss each other, discuss each other. Sometimes the dialogue is awkward. It became clear with this book that my practice in this realm of "collage poems" had begun consolidating. For one thing, it allowed me to "illustrate" (and to propose) political insights and social feelings deep inside that had always been as much a part of my poetry as a cosmological wonder.

AM: To return to the questions of poetics. Your recent work in *Graphic Novella, Works and Days*, and *Numbers* highlights the degree to which you're committed to poetry as a distinctly hybrid form of art making, one that includes any number of different materials and textual forms. As you've continued to push the boundaries of poetry as a medium, what distinctions would you draw now between "poetry" as such and other forms of art? And in the collage that appears in the "Prefaces" section of *Numbers*, you write in longhand and type out the sentence, "Collage is a deictic practice of debris." Could you discuss the importance overall of collage as this sort of "deictic practice of debris" to your work as a poet? And also—to remind us of this, "Making pages" seems a very important concept to the work you've been doing not only of late, but across your career. Could you talk more about making pages and how this inflects the work you and have been doing?

RBD: Well, poetry, as its own particular and saturating language, is emphatically made of words, which includes many dictions, syntaxes, possibilities for segmentivity (in line break for instance), allusions to anything –cultural, political, cosmological, personal. And visual texts are made of images, colors, forms. But both are made of structures, both have vast traditions behind them, and both allude to things (outside, inside). Both poetry and visual arts are therefore deictic (in the double meaning of that word)—they point and they interact positionally. Plus there's the most wonderful tradition of each art form nibbling at each other's borders (there are any number of examples). And that mutual liminality and crossing over has potential that I began to explore. The nibbling part and the increased interactions—where a set of thoughts in one medium sets off dialogue with materials of the other—and then back again are part of what I mean by saying I put the art work on the page and then "read" it. The readings are the poem (at least its beginnings). The "debris" in that aphorism you cited above comes from the desire to see and look by salvaging bits of the almost lost—the almost wasted—it is an ethical position in poetics. And the interactive readings across media challenge me to "make" those interpretable pages with various suggestive seams and junctures. More conventions of seeing/ reading are in play, compounding one's pleasure. "Making pages" is like "making readings," or the potential for readings. It opens more windows via visuality as well as poetry and page space.

In poetry, one wants a rhythmic gathering and confrontation of materials that cause varied emotional and thoughtful responses—an arc of musical on-goingness built by the poem. I used to compare *Drafts* to a string quartet—voices, interactions, clashes, senses of shape made in spacetime by the poem. All this to make a lucid and full experience for the reader. So dialogues of various kinds have always been part of my poetry (as genre, as tonal self-interruptions—lots of ways). I find multiple juxtaposition a good way of negotiating and presenting materials. I like mostly syntactic statements "inside" a single statement, but shifts, change-ups, and juxtapositions in tone, diction, image, affect among the statements (like units, verse paragraphs—that kind of thing). This led me to call what I am doing in poetry "collage." It might also be, a version of the meditative descriptive, or another way of saying seriality.

AM: I'd like to return to a comment you made earlier related to *Graphic Novella*: "It became clearer that doing collage with writing— making that kind of object—-a work of collage-poems as a book— does break the frame of the book, particularly a book of (normal) poems." Could you talk a bit more about this notion of "break[ing] the frame of the book." What's important to you in this move? What new cultural/literary space gets created through this reformation?

RBD: First off—if one does break the frame of a book, all the pages fall out—like sibyl's leaves, and one can begin "making pages" again. This is appealing—the process of consolidating, breaking up, and reinvestigating. There is also something about exploring "the between" that is attractive with any hybrid text. I like the idea of books as a place or zone of a unique event—"reading." I also sometimes call what I am doing in both collage and poetry "making a page." This is why I have literally never gotten over Mallarmé's *Un Coup de Dés* as a visual-dramatic enactment of poetry with page space and typography. I think that the collage poems create a parallel unique hybrid and between space in which to stand. Making that kind of book of the between is a particular pleasure. (It is a little like a self-collaboration.)

AM: I'm struck in *Numbers* in particular of your recent books by the tactile, physical quality of the represented collage pieces included in the book (they're also beautiful!) and the ways in which they align with the verbal poem texts that rest on the opposing pages. Many of the collages date from 2010-2011, but the book was published in 2018. Were you already considering these at the time as part of a book length project that would integrate lineated poetry and image on the page as unified and co-responding art forms? What was involved for you in this process as it unfolded for you over these years?

RBD: Well, yes, I began thinking of making collages that "cited" numbers because I'd found tickets, or had cut a big attractive number from a shopping bag, or had collected other weird debris for collage. I simply started making collages with any given number on it, and a set of these built up over several years (certainly 0, 1 and so on). Stylistically the collages were often self-different and that allowed some of the poems to offer diverse experiences of number (and some phrases about number) on which to comment. Then I am transfixed by pi [π] and the unfathomable mathematics involved in its non-repeating series. "The universe is built on a shim" is one of my awe-struck lines from *Drafts*. All of these began to build into a set and then to a pattern in a series (numbers zero through 5, including pi as a number between 3 and 4) and then a small collection of "etc." The collages began to need poems—a somewhat antic-mysterious need, and these poems became bizarre, amused commentary. No one is further from a mathematician than me. I'm just fascinated by the oddity of the universe.

The process of this work shows two things that often occur in my work—trying to name a project and trying to build or invent a structure for that project. The first would be not just making a few collages with numbers in them—but a desire to make more and then collect them in a set (thus the dates of some collages occur well before the consolidation of the project). The second would be the question how to organize this set; what are the pleasures and the rules for this structure—how will invention present itself?

By the way, and not incidentally, finding someone willing to publish any of these as a collage-poem book in color involves the publisher in an act of amazing enthusiasm and support. I give fervent thanks to Ariel Resnikoff and Julia Warner of Materialist Press (2018). And incidentally, *The Collage Poems of Drafts* by Salt Publishing (2011) were published with a subvention by the Pew Foundation (aid that no longer exits). It remains true that most of the collage poems, conceived as books or chapbooks have appeared mainly in periodicals on-line.

AM: These questions all pertain to *Interstices* (2014), the first book you published after completion of your decades-long project in the long poem, *Drafts*. First, could you talk about this as an "interstitial" work? The word has its origins in the Latin *interstitium*, from *intersistere* 'stand between'. Between what and what is *Interstices* standing? What space or ground is it demarcating as that of the "between" space? I'm here particularly thinking of these lines from "Ledger 7"

> I want the interstices,
> Spatter lines, sketch lines, and cryptograms
> Acting in and on an endless vast excess.
> A splintered apparatus. Babel left in rubble,
> a map of seams as large as large as the remains. (26)

RBD: The lines you cite, looked at retrospectively, could almost describe facing *Drafts* as an entity itself. What happens "between" this poem and something I don't know yet. How to read the "sketch lines" and the "map of seams"? How do I act "in and on an endless vast excess"? Looked at this way, this stanza is touching and comic. But it is also quite intent. If this, then what? it asked. So I dramatized that situation—"a map of seams"—that is, "interstitial."

After *Drafts*, I wanted to become different selves (in poetry) while remaining me. I also wanted to hear further sounds and a brisker poem. In many ways, I was making a big pivot, self-declared, without really having a clue whether projects or a project could occur that were adequate to this time and place. During the next years after 2012, there were qualms, failures, incompletions, nostalgia for the solidity and presence of *Drafts*—you and any empathetic reader can make up a whole list of the nightmares and uncomfortable-ness inherent in not having a clue. Another name for this might be "Second Act Problems." After all, they are not over.

So I thought of all this as an experiment in sound and making, as "interstitial" –as *betweens*, as if I were building a bridge with one pylon (*Drafts*) and an extruding roadway going—but . . . to somewhere? where? and what was both the roadway and the "where"—how even to get "there." Those were some of the queries that I had.

AM: The book *Interstices* is composed as a series of 26 letters to various unnamed individuals, real and/or imagined, signified by individual letters of the alphabet (the number 26 appears as the heading for the two ending poems to this collection). Each of these in turn is preceded by either the title of "ledger" or "letter." First, could you discuss the structural components of this poem in a series of letters and ledgers? Did you have a plan beforehand or did the structure emerge through the writing? Second, what drew you to the epistolary form in this book? What impulses were at work in their composition that provoked this form for this book?

RBD: So to begin again, post-*Drafts*, it was of interest to use a structure like letters—you did always have that 26 to get you somewhere—and to me it double evoked the pun on epistolarity and the alphabetic. It's like the first Ledger is just about addressed to *Drafts* itself as a site, a place, an act in time, and Letter R is clearly to me with the instruction "Leap into your excess/ and compound the crisis" (35). The book is almost like an offering to *Drafts* to help me go on. I do like writing letters (always have), so it felt quite idiomatic and evocative to be writing poems as if addressing friends, acquaintances, frenemies, some poems "about" one person, some about composites. (The initial letters do not indicate the name of the person, except rarely.) And between the letters were "ledgers," meaning some accounting, here of time, place and situation. So an alternating structure came to me, with some sense of a double dialogue—between me and the addressee (who was also a "letter" of the alphabet), and between each letter and an "account" in a ledger, with some sense of time, also specific sites, zones, or places. That why, in the ledger poems there are a certain number of cosmological poems ("outer space" –is it a time? or a place? Well, it's kind of both.) And the time/place of a poem, of the dead, of travel, and of dreams also appear in the Ledger poems.

I had no particular plan when I began, but one soon arrived. You know I like to do what I call "projecting a form." (My other phrase like that is "projecting a project"—often said to students back in that day.) That would be making some kind of composite satisfying shape for this particular assemblage of feelings and practices. Making one's work is making a form for one's work at the same time. It was a way of taking account---of where I was. Of renewing a pledge—to poetry. That sense of its necessity I try to keep in mind (as I say in Letter 13). Words are "not enough./ One must name the shadows/ of something unhearable,/ the activated void, the blue./ Name oneself and others/ name our time/ and name the stakes/ of thought" (49). The sound (to my ears) still does have some of the feeling of *Drafts*. That is because *Interstices* was like a mini-version of the whole book *Pledge/Précis* (*Drafts 39-57* with the unnumbered poem), consisting of poems dedicated to friends (not necessarily the same ones in both books).

I thought at this point that all the books (to come) would be describable as interstitial, and had an insight that they would all be "connected" to *Drafts* as if tied to the tapestry of that large work as extra related parts of the site sculpture—more bits of "fabric art." to extend the large work or put odd kinds of book-length glosses or footnotes as attachments to *Drafts*. This was a good thought for a while. But as the projects multiplied, something shifted, and that one metaphor of "addenda" and extra bits tied on became obsolete.

(I liked that textile metaphor, by the way; it was a useful provisional visualization of Big Structure.)

As it turned out, in another Big Structure, my roadway "found" the other pylon of the bridge and didn't just hang forever over the water.... What seemed possible, by about 2014 was a different kind of long poem in book-length episodes, called *Traces, with Days.* Books of traces, books of days, and some definitional thinking about <what do I mean>. This is what I am doing now, along with related books of collage poems we just talked about, that are independent of *Traces, with Days.* (In that set, three titles have been published so far, up to 2020.) Given this, I sometimes think of my poetic career as occurring backwards—doing the Big Poem first, then accomplishing an array of shorter books.

AM: Insofar as counting and numbering appear here as constitutive facts of daily observation, *Interstices* seems to be reckoning in particularly acute ways with the passing of time, mortality, aging. Of course, these are longstanding tropes in poetry, so there's nothing new in that. But the reckoning with death in *Interstices* (as in *Late Work*) has a deeply situated, material, and decidedly non-elegiac feel to it. I was particularly struck by these lines from "Ledger 6" in which you write:

> There was an obituary the other day that
> counted the person's total minutes.
> General first-world average is: 34, 790, 757.
> Even coming in at over thirty-four million,
> it's a chilling account. It all adds up, but
> still I'm afraid to calculate my stats. (22)

It's a deeply funny and at the same time frightening scenario, but also one firmly rooted in the numerical position of a lifetime, counted up—with no infinity but an end stop, in this case the 34, 790, 758th minute. I wonder if you could reflect on what are sincere gestures toward mortality, the human, ones that feel shaped by a fiercely compassionate human accounting.

RBD: I think you've answered your own questions with the words compassionate and sincerity—and the amused feeling. One cannot help but notice mortality happening in all directions. A particular reason for me is, after spending a "career lifetime" inside one poem, then going on to other interesting projects, I would like to maximize my time to be here and see what happens with these projects. And at this moment (2020, at a time inside a world-wide pandemic that is being handled in the US about as badly as possible), one cannot help but have compassion for oneself and others who are caught in interior exile, yet having to act within the limits of a historical event into which they have been swept up—commandeered, really.

AM: Much of your poetry seems an effort to envision a world without the formations of cultural injustice so embedded in our own. I have in mind your essay, "Autobiography from 1998 and 2016," in which you include two poems, the first written in 1998 as a letter and the second, written in 2016 specifically for the journal in which this piece was published, that comments on and responds to the earlier "you" from 20 years back. At one point in a section from the 2016 poem, you comment, "My aesthetic crisis is my political crisis." Could you expand on this statement in context of your recent post-*Drafts* work?

RBD: That is a citation from a friend, Amze Emmons, printmaker. It was germane! You're asking how did you make some of this work (tactics) and what are the overarching poetics—loosely implied as a "political poetics" or even better, socio-cosmological. You have begun with a dynamic in my works inside the poetry, as the poetry, in fact as the very texture of the poetry that comments on events, the state of the world all as part of its forms, its subject matter and its ethos. It is difficult to talk about this because the poetics is not settled; it is always in a self-probing process.

The shifting around of an aesthetic sense (which is never just aesthetic!) I attribute to the 21st century (on the tail of the rather unpalatable 20th), with the final wake-up call being the strangeness of living in a pandemic in which our much-vaunted national systems and institutions are under great stress, or under stress more widely recognized than in the past. We are not who we think we are. (These institutions were already were suffering slippage, cracks, problems, dysfunctions for at least decades of social dis-investment and ideological push; it's certainly not acceptable to see them as still functioning for most public good, particularly under recent years of no upkeep.) That is, we live within an accelerated socio-political and economic crisis. Many people, including me, can no longer settle time, air, rooms, food, insight. One response is trying to evaluate my art—does it stand up well in light of all we have gone through in recent months. Can I go further writing about our long-term chronic crisis with any further exploration of aesthetic-social questions and tactics? I don't mean "writing about" COVID—I generally do not write "about" but inferentially. And—this is not meant as a footnote—after our engagement with this interview, the repressed crisis of racial injustice in the US burst out into the open, finally and again, with results still to occur (stated on June 16, 2020). It is a characteristic of periods of enormous shift that yesterday's news is obsolete almost as soon as it is registered.

What this feels like in a literary way is that my "aesthetic crisis *remains* my political crisis." I have never felt that the aesthetic act of writing excluded social observations/ materials. What does one write about if these are peremptorily excluded? It is our very specific culture that says the aesthetic and "political" (particularly any contemporary observations) are opposite-binaries. I literally do not comprehend this and what it entails, but I know it is a deeply unspoken yet quite active assumption for many poets; to me it is a pallid limiting thought. For all relationships as depicted in poetry, all meditations on just about anything have a social and "political" aspect—perhaps offered in fable, allegory or indirection. I am trying different ways to explore and express this feeling of crisis and meaning. The intermingling of these two aspects of being in the world (aesthetic and political—in shorthand) occurs repeatedly, is not settled, is re-evoked whenever poetry, visual text, collage, essay are being roiled up and evoked in me. What I *can* say (because you locate this as post-*Drafts* work) is that *Drafts is* about many of these materials, and that sometimes I look at that work (1986-2012) and feel like Cassandra. I already noted that my sense of a crisis accelerating started becoming larger and more unmanageable after 2012—and is true even beyond the pandemic.

AM: The terms "experimental" and "avant-garde" have increasingly been questioned for their adequacy and purpose in relation to contemporary poetry. How useful and/or appropriate do you find such designations for your work as a poet today?

RBD: This question, too, is not easily settled. I am made very uncomfortable by and resistant to labels like *avant-garde* or *experimental,* because I instantly think of exceptions. As easy short-hand terms they can be useful, but not otherwise. So my answer would be that the terms are situational, maybe only comparative (in relation to what else we are looking at when we use these terms), historically applicable by meaning or designating specific moments or objects in a time-frame or for specific uses. That is, say, 30 years ago, one of those terms might have been very exciting. Perhaps now "experimental" is interesting as stating not using conventional or familiar solutions (or even thoughts). The word should not indicate mannerisms that becomes a period style, a rhetoric of currently agreed-on stylistic traits to signal to a cohort. The term avant-garde has a military flair, comes from a war context, and claims, for all these cutting-edge soldiers in a (non-bloody) war of artistic practices, the positive aura of a "struggle" where you make an incursion and hit strongly for some strategic goal. This term seems to borrow from actual war and actual revolution and work by a simple (maybe even pallid) analogy--as wars of words and positions. The avant-garde claims it is "ahead of the times"—but you can't be ahead of your times—no matter, you are "inside" your times. After that suspicion, then add that avant-garde to me has come to mean either too charmingly in the know and almost insincere (doing things for outward effects, not for thinking in your art), sometimes rigid with program, possibly prone to developing a "style" or "manner" to distinguish oneself just for that distinction, market-artful and even narcissistic or unreadable—by this time, after this list, I am convinced I am a philistine.

Frankly, reading needs to be nimble, curious and tolerant. There are numerous historical versions of the avant-garde and their experiments—basically these can be consumed or identified or named as "schools" or as poetics—Beat poetics, New York School, surrealism, high modernism—and you can derive various working poetics from various extrapolations of traits manifested by key poems in those formations. There's a lot of extraction involved in this. Sometimes one notices manifestos and then reads poems as "conforming" to those manifestos (but doesn't notice contradictory, mixed-up moves). These normalizing readings are educational and pedagogic. BUT (as Susan Rosenbaum noted) these self-confirming acts of extrapolation can be very hard on people not counted as central to the culture (politically, racially, gender-ly rather outside or to the side), who are generally not in those movements but may make their own art on their terms. Even "Experiment" can become a self-enclosed, self-confirming circle. So if you talk about experiment--and you can do this pretty accurately via these "named" or already named poetics or groups or tendencies, you aren't being critically experimental; you might still miss people who don't fit, or who "don't count." For a long time, women were in that marginalized "second-rated" situation, with rare exceptions. I've written about this a good deal as a critic, trying to help construct a literary history with women poets IN it, not called inadequate, lacking, immature, unnecessary, without authority, or too brassy, outspoken, unsubtle, emotional, etc. I call my reading strategy a "feminist reception" that is—THE WRITERS don't have to be feminist, but I do, in order to study the forces of production, dissemination [sic], reception. This reading strategy pays attention to women, but also to male varietals, gender marginal, African American, queer people, anti-masculinist folks, those historically "off-center" and their literary choices and agency, particularly investigating their experiments—narratively, socially, aesthetically in all sorts of mixes. And feminist reception was pretty experimental in reading this work, by analyses NOT using normal benchmarks of power, judgment, and accepted understanding of tone or syntax or any elements of form.

AM: In the 2011 "Ur-scene, ur-new: The History of the Longpoem and the 'Collage Poems of *Drafts*,'" [jacket2.org/feature/drafting-beyond-ending] Ron Silliman describes you as a "rationalist....who is completely committed to exploring that razor edge where language becomes something else, whatever that may be." Would you agree with Silliman's assessment of you and your work? In what ways do you see your post-*Drafts* explorations as showing us something new about the ways in which "language becomes something else"?

RBD: Well, I like the word "committed." It is always strange when someone decides to sum you up—and this was at the conference for my retirement, so it was a rhetorical move to make after my four decades of professional career. If by "rationalist," he meant trying to think clearly and not be too self-deceived—OK. Now I had to look up "rationalist" again to remember—does he mean "not spiritual"—well, I feel cosmological in outlook—and that's a lot of Beyond and its principles of the unknown right there. I do try not to "believe in authority" (says the dictionary), but c'mon! there is a limit to that. I tend toward skepticism, but still you need to act in the world as a real choice, even in an "as if" way. Does he mean not flappy, having some authority? Like everyone, not always. So I don't "get" that word as a descriptor, but Ron has a good turn of generalizing sometimes, so every once in a while, I think—why did he say that? Does he mean that I can write in argument and I can also write divagations and loops (and the best is mixing the two)?—That turned out to be true across my career, but I had to grow into and develop the ability. But I *would* admire someone who is always trying for "language to become something else" while staying language—expanding its horizons, one might say, thickening its richness and implications, seriousness and wit. If that's me—OK.

AM: In "+53" from *Around the Day in 80 Worlds* you write:

"Poetry can extend the document."

Addendum: poetry might also constitute
the document.

The quotation is from Muriel Rukeyser's serial, documentary poem, *U.S. 1* [1938]. The use of Rukeyser here seems important, as is your addendum. Similarly, in a poem from *Late Work*, you write of "aphorism, paradoxes and / fragments" that could be

strung together as if a continuous text

to document something
of what we are seeing
(even with blind spots)

Could you expand on your sense of the document and documentation as these concepts relate to your thinking and writing as a poet?

RBD: I do not want to decorate my age; I want to investigate it, to explore it, feel through it and notice. Language evoking feeling-thought of the most granular sort is the "tool" for that investigation, so too is the invention of big shapes, intensive form—something responsive to the largest-smallest sense of the socio-cosmological. Sometimes that sense of document just means a tiny person standing amid history and the universe and looking around.

"Document" or the acts around documenting, noticing, and accounting might point to my choice to use newspaper clippings in both *Graphic Novella* and *Days and Works*, where some are droll, some are tragic, some, one just goes "oh, look" or "are they kidding?"—referring to things happening at times and places in which one is currently saturated. I cite the back of an upscale water bottle alongside reportage of a polluted water source used by a family and their toddler in *Days and Works*. This strategy is not intended to be a dose of right-thinking information as a curative pill that you are given by Dr. Poetry—these citations in and as texts are mingled with my words and together generate a sense of recognition and co-immersion. The incredible mixed feelings one lives all day. I have framed the question in *Days and Works* "How can so many things occupy the same space?"--including page space. The result is shock, warmth, rage, all inter-interrupted, heteroclite and painful. This has made the eclectic a characteristic of my work. I write big and small in scale; I use rhyme or don't; I deploy both asyntactic collage and syntactic materials; my work is both paratactic and hypotactic; it can be continuous in statement but also fragmented into leaps; it can end and also at other times be open-ended.

Another parallel tactic to "document" might be my citing ephemera (handouts; instructions; political flyers) in the category of "gray literature"—like using a handout of the dress code from visiting a prison, this embedded in my work verbatim, near or involved with my own words, observations and comments. Facts and documents, when resituated, can be quite striking and informative (as Williams knew) by connecting situations, events or juxtaposing mind-sets you hadn't noticed before. *Graphic Novella* has that intention, as we saw, taking observations, poetry, aphorisms, prose poems, accounts, photographs, diagrams all sequenced together as a form of "documentation."

Another work you asked about is the notational book *Around the Day in 80 Worlds*. Oddly, the book was written when "I could not write"—what I was seeing in the world and just observing was so odd, ordinary and off-putting (I was living through a major heat wave and drought) that I was almost paralyzed. A title, taken from someone else, actually, started to organize terse, suggestive, experiential aperçus. Sequencing—how to get emotionally (or intellectually) from one thing to another—is a tactic for my writing and was in play in this work. (I wrote many more than eighty little sections, and then carved and sequenced this work to that exact number, with an allusion that we all know from Verne, which is where Cortázar found it for his compendium.)

I have a projected set of books, *Traces, with Days*—to which a lot of this recent work belongs. One mode is notational books of *Days*—and curiously the titles are all, to date, borrowed—from Hesiod, from Cortázar, and (next possibly) from Dennis Tedlock. The books of *Traces* will alternate with the *Days*. *Late Work* (conceived of as a text of traces, constructed as poems) was published in 2020. It appears that I have projected a long-poem in book-length episodes under this rubric, something that continues and somewhat matches *Drafts*. But I don't want to get ahead of myself—this is, as *Drafts* was, a heuristic project, learning by doing, the poetics as much under construction as the books.

With all this, you asked in effect, are these all part of a genre called "document." Is this a "documentary" poetics? Well really there's only one "genre" for all this—poesis or making, or, to say it another way, there are many plausible and pleasurable genres from ode to doggerel. Some are thought of as "more poetic"; insofar as the term "document" means only slightly poetic, it interests me as stating an attitude. I am fond of using odd genres (as in *Drafts*, alphabets, haibun—this not so rare, now—codas, prefaces). But the only

genres to present in even one work now for me are mixes: multiple
and polyphonous—a mélange, heterogeneric bundle—lyric
and document and aphorism, and fable and journey (etc).

"Document" needs to be an intimate, thought-laden "document."
I mean, you walk through life and you run into events, ideas,
insights, things seen, and conversely events and people (and so
forth) run into you, and you try to think about all of this by making
works. A poem is also going to "document" languages, many social
heteroglossias. So, language and the invention of forms and material
create statement, and so too statement creates forms. It is the
endless dialogue of poesis—of making. We have talked about my
idea of "making pages" to think of the poetics I want with the poems,
implicating the genre Book in and as poesis. My ethos is probably
like the two deictics, the pointing words that lie at the heart of *Drafts*:
IT and IS.

Song of the Andoumboulou: 285

Nathaniel Mackey

All the birds had called a conference, they
   were on their phones in a conference
call, awake chattering no matter the leaves'
                             lull-
   aby. They had left tracks in the dirt we
     called writing, by which we meant song was
the same as ongoingness, not what was but
                             what
   carried. They met on bent boughs in the
woods of the beloved or the woods that were
   the beloved, loath of late to say which…
                        Being
loath was what being a bird again meant, in-
   to its mystic circularity they went, we the
migrating they. Again it felt good to be birds
                      again,
   at large in an alien place no matter, the demi-
   urgic shakedown we were caught up in no
matter. We looked on as two lovers wiped spit
                    from

their lips, ripening toward crux, toward crisis,
toward chaos, having kissed promulgating the
ephemeral witness they were thereby afforded.

A

distillation of living they called it. The birds
were all on their phones about it but no one batted
an eye. Such exactly was the way of the realm...
So as to be of a feather we as well would not bat

an

eye. "Bird, be my best or my better," we each
intoned, loose cloth we wore commanding the
flown ones aflutter, the proper ones no matter

we'd

never be. Choral we insisted it be seen as no
matter, that one eventuate many, animacy's miracle,
music a kind of profligacy but apt. It was only a

meet-

ing of the birds we were or the birds we'd be, hum-
mingbird to muni, all stripes, the strip or the stretch
made of the loose-fitting cloth we wore, so wanted

were

we, so sage and so sought after... Many a quill
went into the writing of *The Book of So*, many a
plucked feather. *Refried* came out *rarified* and had

to

be crossed out, many a bottle of ink went dry.
We looked out from the woods into Arjuna's world,
a threat of reprisal stalled atop it like smoke, en-
mity molecular so deep it went. The lovers with spit

on

their lips loomed large and stood their ground, much
more than meat between dingy teeth we now in-
sisted, partway between proper and flown, Krishna's

aco-

lytes, black ones to be. It all had to do with it we
fell back knowing, insisting we knew as though for the
first time, as good as it felt to be birds again not to

be

looked at askance... It all had to do with it, the it that

was all and the all that was the it of it, a late deriv-
ative we coaxed into wholeness as we could, the birds

                                                        we

    had became or we would be. Not since before when
we were birds had we had it so good, no matter good
accompanied bad or grew out of it sometimes we now

                                                    knew.

    The it it all had to do with leaned in like angular
affection, an oblique sweetness the lovers proved right
    about. Choral we insisted it be seen as, the we we'd

                                                        be,

"no matter" a mantra
now

                        •

    Each and every lady wore a Levi's jacket atop
a sun dress. Andreannette's ex's pea coat was
a thing of the past each of them thereby said, so

                                                    of

    a feather they'd be. So as to espouse a middle
truth, we were later told, many a middle truth, the
    soft rigor of denim had been brought into play.

                                                    We

    insisted it be seen as choral, not that it needed
our insistence but that it behooved us, rough edge
    to rough edge, to so align… They were each a

                                                bird,

as in featherlight, cipherlike in what was other-
    wise number, a cryptographic something seen in
a face or the shape of a calf, writing one could see

                                                    but

    not read. Something seen in the slope of the nape
of a neck likewise, a tarjuman whose legend one lacked.
    Animacy's miracle had its way with us was what it

                                                    was,

    the way it had of moving like mercury what it was…
It was this too the birds were on their phones about.
    I looked on wanting one myself, wanting a phone of

my own. It was as much the phone as the bird I'd be

an

  ardency inside me clamored for. I was looking in
    and I was looking out, a bird and a bird-to-be both.
Each of them and each of us was of a feather and a

rare

  bird as well, no matter how choral it was as well as
exactly how choral it was. All we knew and all they
  knew was that all the birds had called a conference

and

they were on their phones in a conference call, tweets
  only so many words now as well as words only so
many tweets... It was all we could do not to know the

dif-

  ference, one feather flush against another no match,
all not to wrinkle a page in *The Book of So*. It was no
  longer enough to say "So it was" or "So it went," one's

head

  secretly housed under a sun dress, one's head's harvest
  contraband. One stood birdheaded, only partly the
bird one would someday be. "Toward Birdness" went

the

  new chapter's title, a chapter we sat surrounding as
  well as a chapter we sat around in, not to be erased or
written over, an ibis no matter one might be. Choral we insist-
ed again it was or it would be, all of it accruing to the one

yet

again... "All I ever wanted," we heard one of the spit-driven
  lovers explain, "was to be at the moment's beck and call,
beyond duration, beyond death," said with the ring of a vow

and

  a confession, one's right to break up or break down there-
by affirmed. Lyrical beauty sponsored brass recalcitrance
  we heard in the background music we imagined, imaginal
sound's own suzerainty the realm we were now in, a place

we

  had been before. The Offshore Brass had come ashore it
sounded like, "like" an aspect static attended or attached

itself to, sputter and spurn planted but to be inferred, the

im-

   plicate order's demur... Each of the ladies projected
torque and containment, a light grace the denim jacket lent
   rough and ready notes, an akimbo aspect pressed or im-
plied. It all conveyed continuance ratcheting down, chemise

mere

   horizon, muted amplitude, we the about-to-be birds the
migrating they all the while we looked on. They were no more
   they than they were we, we no more we than we were they,

all

   the mystique of who had what no mystique, the intrigue
no intrigue, to be choral testified as much. All the birds had
   called a conference and were on their phones in a conference

call

   we knew for sure, soon-come surely come, decidedly the way
   it would be and the way it was. Tweets were only so many
words now, words only so many tweets, ends exactly nothing if

not

means

•

Bodily retreat had me sipping wine in Wrack Tavern.
   The horizon line cut like a knife in the distance,
my body's inner jihad a cellular war with itself, so

far

   from the abandoned boy's beloved beach. Bodily
perfection had hit like a dagger in the eye, the ladies'
   light cotton under denim a caution, long since no

long-

   er acted on... I heard the hoopoe's chatter. I heard
the swallow. I heard them all. I was a bird or I was
   about to be. It wasn't that I eavesdropped. All the

birds

had called a conference, they were on their phones in
   a conference call. I was a bird or I was about to be,
I heard them all. "So it was" or "So it went" lay way

be-

hind me, the charmed or enchanted circularity of it
moot. Nothing would be given us I knew, it all hav-
  ing to do with it having no exit or escape, phatic res-
cue were there rescue at all... What I wanted was to

                                                    ray

  out in all directions, my own heliocentric sun, less
    a bird who flew too close than a bird abdicating its
feathers, a way of being more than one place at once.
I was feeling the wind between my teeth and liking it.

                                                      I

  washed it down with Sidi Brahim. Wine scoured my
insides going down and when it got to my stomach,
  an emptiness it scrubbed and went on with. All it was

                                                  was

  I was killing time. What it was was I was waiting
for the hammer to fall. A diffuse bodiliness was our only
  hope I felt, border, though it might, on bodilessness,

                                                soul

said to be a bird or to fly like a bird, soul said to be gone
  or to've never been... It would be an all-at-once meeting,
neither flesh nor feather, an all-on-our-phones-all-at-once

                                                      con-

  gregation, akin to or a kind of shared mind or spirit, not
so remote, not so abstract... It would be all the birds hav-
  ing called a conference, all the birds on their phones in a

                                                    con-

ference
call

We bent over reading tracks in the dirt, a new
book known as *The Soon Book* unfolding we thought,
maybe less book than scroll. It was a back-when

                             mood
   it put us in. Chicken-scratch guitar had nothing
on any of us, the jook band or the chorale we'd
   be… Zygodactyl tracks made a music we could

                             see
but not hear, we who'd have been birds or were
   soon to be birds, we with our magnifying glasses
walking around in boots… Had it not already had

                             to
   do with it, it would all have to do with it. Had it
already, it all had to do with it, a way it had of having
   its way or the way the wind had, not a needle nor a

                             leaf

not trem-
bling

Two Poems

Maurice Scully

Glimpse

Dusting air with yr right hand
to make what's left
right, & on a good day, better ...
Death – Sex – Memory – Regret –
throw the dice – what else next? Click.
Suddenly on a good day, young again,
you *get* it, left to right, left to right
itself into that dream of what's deemed
perfect, that dark inheritance you happen
to be heir to, that little trickling river of life ...
le chiave, se notlolo, na heochracha.
And write a poem about it.
In the summer of 1939 the poet Robert Lax
looked up into the sky of New York City
& saw jet-trails threading across from
building to building – dapple of windowglass –
jagged sirens – flags – pigeons – crowds –
& seeming to spell out he said, vividly, on
Patmos, fifty years later, a limber elder to this
young Irish eejit by the sea, the word Pax.

Chink

But those double images always
remained mysterious   how?

pictures   intensity

translatable into

outside the words the

sound peels off the poetry

crumbled

on the floor

of the empty

gallery. Echo. A dust.

That's it.

But not quite.

Is this then that bright outline of a matrix,
of a "radiating primacy of the invisible"
that I used to contemplate, wide-eyed,
blind, in kindergarten-college for the tubby
drunken hero-professor? I lift a finger & notice
a star outside a window in a space of fictional
energy it seems/dreams he must now hand
over to you, you there taking that last step
beginning your descent by the backstairs to
the alleyway below. Sirens, lights. A field of
weaving energies that peels off, softly descending
to cover a corner of your precious western
imagination a moment then dissolve into
the brainstem. NFS.

Yes. Maybe.

Maybe Yes

Seasons

Peter Hughes & Eléna Rivera

The following poems are taken from a collaboration between Peter and Eléna that lasted from November 2019 to October 2020. The poems respond to each other, but also to the solo piano suite *Les Saisons* by Tchaikovsky.

November

> turning into strangers in the flat above
> the clocks go back
> along the rutted tracks
>
> through forests
> of the unimagined
> chestnut music
>
> chrysanthemum dusk
> at only twenty five to
> home made pumpkin soup
>
> offerings to convalescent skies
> an overpowering smell of more flags
> burning in the plaza

(PH)

November

can't turn back the clocks

pattern of the profligate

flags memories in cold November

air music's light offering vanished

breathless

now legs, arms, body stiffen

in unseasonably chilly efforts

unimagined previously a pose rutted in repetition

bluing the familiar restoration: "move"

shade of coral days

and trees the autumnal flower

seen now beyond windowpanes

translucent and shy now what sense wasn't squandered

the immigrant's prison-bars at dusk

a handful of how to's

(ER)

December

> heavy skies are roosting
> in the holly & the oak
> the tallest & least visible

> loads are suddenly lit up
> exactly now
> acidic & yet crystalline
> refractions of the light

> through water turning
> in & out of us & ice
> with metamorphoses of memory
> zoom out from its little cage fighters
> to non-figurative drips & flickers

> into pathways trodden
> by these strange arrivals
> carrying the echoes

> of a party in the distance
> becoming fainter
> as they carry us away

(PH)

December

A death is announced (as in a mystery)
Prickly winds, flowers for a girl killed—
rapid transformation of form (from on high)

Approaching Winter Equinox, a date
doubling as light-post in all that cold rain
Let's make a list, clear the day drinking

Left the world with no memory (just mystery)

Nature is going/has gone to sleep (a bit of noir
inside and out) "The Affair Of" the whodunit

Small words brush in what the man called
the "narrow language" at a talk on poetry
and translation, a bit of tin being siblings

"A lie to stop pain" threads the mind
Twilight comes early, doesn't sit as easily
in the body a place of termination or free-fall

(ER)

January

> the earth's stuffed crust
>   is scorched
>   & from the top
> of the revolving restaurant
>   we're granted glimpses
>   of incinerated
>   foreigners & forest
> heaps of tangible marsupials
>   the softly blackened outlines
>   now dismembered
>   by the winds that fanned
>   by failure
>   roar throughout the night

(PH)

January

a moment in the middle of the last
will I redress after a season of shifts
the remaining day in tomorrow's snow
forget the plan the thought of books

the pages when in winter the snow's
heavy on evergreens ink on a page
accumulates thoughts of elsewhere
link the forest to seared absent selves
freed briefly of my sonant habitation
write to Tchaikovsky's *The Seasons*
and hope I can see look in front of me
not frolic in the future lurking that trial
that binds to the earth even more debris
that grows breeds in the cold white sky
the space between shadow and light I
see from this window a photograph there
in my mind on this cold day the portrait
of "it is"—is it real or the island voice
that counts time tries to find what light
is where it's for sale where it comes from
how in the end details surface in a city
wracked with speed and future forward
lead here where time stops for a moment
in the midst of the last lifting of space
and the enduring project: "how we see it"

(ER)

February

    here's another unelected twilight
granular as in an old Italian volume
            roosting in the clock with one hand shadowed

    by the other
  wing is crudely carved
         as if by orphans

      emulating other people's parents making
    simple spoons with grandma's hatchet
          & an elbow of storm birch

the transformed green wood drying on the porch
where is has now turned dark
we know the feeling
(PH)

February

Back again from snow covered arched alleys of pine and birch
to jack hammers breaking pavement whipping up a rough kind of time—

knots we hold in our stomach just because we desired, so chin up
that sweet turn has transformed into a rod to punish inside outside.

See me now the frog just about to jump into the pond! Look!
Have I made a splash? Splash! Splash! Plop! Here's the flash

in the pan I set up, tied me up, then scrambled in different directions.
I say no in my mind and yes with my tired vocal chords—Poor Tom

waiting at South Station about to embark on a new novel eating cold bacon.
The Palestinian actress and a restless spirit pacing back and forth, poor heart,

train pulling out of the station, did we get the right ticket? Printing them
out because we couldn't quite trust our cellphones which we clutched at.

We became close for a day sharing the ride with time and impatience
on our way to where those who have made the numbers compose comfort.

The last experience disappears with the sound of the steel and rubber,
countryside passing, more buildings appearing, a return to chopped up

time and the next appointment where a woman will prod this time
and we'll wonder together if it was all worth it this measuring of the flesh.

I'll wear my yellow vest and let you guess to the kind I am referring to,
I'm a-cold and you my ticket will lead me to "night and day beginning again."

(ER)

March

  a longer evening light begins to play
across the damp catchments of the valley
  & these eyelash fractals of resistance

the king is in his armoured counting house
  & has proclaimed that fire should be allowed
free reign to ransack woods & villages

  so as to reinforce the commonwealth's
immunity to future conflagration
  the slightly longer evening light plays on

around our temporary clearing
  a hint of fresh petal on the blackthorn
& a pair of long-tailed tits are building

(PH)

Mars

How to write of the present
          Daylight savings time thrust forward
new light—this season now "pandemic"

Stillness descends, city crocus
          bloom daffodils between empty
towers, some still work, having to—

having to move forward this month
          ruled by Ares in the Western Canon—
social distancing dilates, isolates

"And it's only been one week" he said
          laughing—third month, year 2020
Stymied as gods extend the days

Self-isolation and soon in lockdown
        as the number of cases in N.Y. rise—
the propulsion of that rhythm forward

The population acclimates to crisis
        City birds chirp, trees burgeon,
high tech trills and sirens fill the air
                         sirens   sirens

(ER)

April

so everybody's backing up
& burying their cheeses

some nights it's harder
to decide

die behind a skip

        or dance in front of thousands
to Tchaikovsky

(PH)

April

Did I mention
Did I mention pace
A generation hesitating
To fill the blue with attention

Hit the pot hard enough
They'll all see you, even on TV
There's that desire for lilacs
To scream, and dance

A few sleep til two
And find the slumber
Of melancholia leaning in
Like an empty street
Gardens blocked off

Still waiting for a shepherd
Who chose the music
The keys are in what chord
Did I mention procreation

Cry now that you can't stray
With a heart empty of future
Fish it out from the well
The tree and trauma still
For now, did I mention …

(ER)

May

            the instrument
        communicates
      across the years of light
       the years of darkness
            Hubble ultra deep field images
              ways the past remains
            remote & palpable
            implacable & hard
          to calculate
         these musics or
      the modulus of rupture
         for the self
             the neighbours
                  & the state

(PH)

May
> **Nights**

The quiet of a city in quarantine, brisk
winds, then a pause, then a slight breeze
noticing the notes of memory on a piano
glide—taste the ginger in your mouth

Scribe now of direct experience not
now a moment of consolation near
starlight—don't let me leave this place,
the white nights of this swaying season

Trees certainly can be playful in the dark
sway in the movement of the evening
inflorescence gone with the rain though
the water keeps the merry dripping high

A rolling residence in liquid introspection
A gazelle's gift as thoughts fly over trees
this season, with or without seasoning
the greening of lambent skies at dusk

as we precipitate toward our patterns
pondering our passage, slowing down
movement from a rapid romantic rise to
wave as you traverse an entire experience

(ER)

June

> Giovanni Bellini reflections
> ripple through the surfaces of
> autumn in an empty wooden frame
>
> duck through a hole in the wall
> & follow the course of the stream
> uphill as far as the lake
>
> watermarks through consciousness
> eradicated olive trees
> eradicated settlement
>
> La Madonna dell'Orto
> open now
> closes 5.30

(PH)

June

not so much "becoming" the instrument
        impervious to time I write a list of protests
                until I forget something resonant in the heat

a piano boating song washes over sirens
        the combat just as fierce inside as outside
                a witness at home marking time like Crusoe

curfew on the imagination—the theme masked
        something about the sequence, transmission
                breathing in one theatrical image after another

a carpenter bee nests in the wood chair
        Rapunzel in her tower writes notes to still
                the noise, the curtain rises while unpacking

(ER)

July

I thought I heard Hart Crane murmur
     in the mind's sound
     through wires that modulated
     to the ghost of a mazurka
     in a lost line of Jack Spicer
or the insides of a broken radio
     in an empty Welsh hotel room
     where the song of someone else's
     lost companion & the ashes of
     forgotten gods sift downwards
through the twisted frames of pines & limes
     & carbonised imagined architecture
     to paraphrase the thinking
     which is rumblestrip glistening
     opposite plus waves & cats nearly
noiselessly steering through one fence
     then another across these
     moonlit gaps in cloud
     over hills to the east the stars
     are haunting three uninhabited planets
boots on gravel & the death of freedom

(PH)

July

The history of calamity or
the fragrant amber of the squash flower

Notes can be heard in the holes
"I hear the notes" trickle

Who drew the map?
Who made the border we are tethered by?

The gun, the fireworks, in season
What will you grill with that?

Most of the birds fled, but I'm here
parched in the summer sun

Ghosts in high rise forests
incrust towering echoes

(ER)

July (Version 2)

Fragrant amber summer sun

                                        surface anticipation

                                        in season

                                        tethered by

                                        calamity

"I hear the notes" we are

                                        in this country

                                        invisible ghosts

                                        towering echoes

The border made

high-rise history

Fireworks incrust

and most birds flee

but I'm here

framed

August

storms have rinsed
the trees the virus is
discouraging some tourists
in the middle
of the woods
there is no middle
of the woods
just an underlying
conversation joining
all these species
like a tawny owl
sat slowly owling
thoughts of tree
in tree slowly
grow over half
a dozen centuries
more seconds pass &
I remember
I must remember bread

while early evening
is creating bark rubbings
of consequent sounds
in floaters & this
translucent halo
posterior
vitreous detachment
an unmanned track
goes on ascending
to the first or last
of the Carneddau
descending to the river

(PH)

August

time doesn't stop
August sings
        a quick melody

a moment's translation
that anticipates sights of
        the rose-breasted grosbeak

where mind gets lost
in the tangle gives permission
        for the moment to echo

fast forward an Evening
Primrose opens only at twilight
        lost in a yellow description

the overflow of pine birch
maple that moment where
        what is near is so brief

resistance to the word

that captures Green Mountains
        mirrored in the flat lake

can't describe the harvest
the virus keeps families away
        gestures culled by the mind

crickets announce fall
twists and turns of perception
        future an approach fast forward

back to city narratives like
"Who lives, who dies"
        without benefit of allegory—

(ER)

September

we followed Elen of the Ways
into September with the hunt
rampaging in our heads
the line of fire advancing
through the forest
we thought about what happens
to the rain
the spore & languages
the individual notes
migratory & tidal
exceptional & accidental
phonemes lodged in feathers
the vowel in down
the stranded scraps
accumulate & nest
around the drowned

(PH)

September

      Saw the land
                 ignite
One thing, then another
               Who saw the wind?

Fire   Flood   Virus
               At the crossroad
                  And we're all stuck in our
boxes

      Beaten by our constant need   /   Even if it all falls apart

Dis-moi, je suis là
               "Who has seen the wind?"
What's next?
What's the rush?
                  to look for meaning, bitter-

      sweet "folds of feeling"
               Land nowhere
                    pass by

        Who counts the numbers

                    Clouds pass in a blue
sky

(ER)

October

what about   I don't know   maybe
Slow Motion Blackbird by Chris Hughes
to go along with the Tchaikovsky
as the rain is softly falling
in the radio & over all these mountains

woods & buildings people's lives uneasily
co-existing with the branded news receptors
another acorn knocks on this thin cabin roof
the autumn oak leaves wonder when to fall
but this is when I make a brand new start
I'm calling it *The Modulus of Rupture*
a book of poems that might not see the light of day
but it's good to have a project
that doesn't fuck up an entire country
or world if you include the run up
well it's true that a lot of dreams these days
feel pretty tame compared to modern film
or politics & news of yet another death
Les says they used to make the coffins out of elm
as it was more hospitable to bugs & fungi
& so settled into other modes of life
sooner than some of us expected
this wet day began again with an exemplary blackbird's song
& this is just a temporary break

(PH)

October

What about
dawn drops
turn day
into a volatile
companion
a thrush
shakes
in the rain
rubbed, swept up
the art of
looking forward to
form
rustling leaves
crackle, raucous

in the wind, rain
a helicopter roams
in Harlem skies
Sigh
history in miniature
hidden
from ourselves
shaped
by four walls
the wee body
is lost
lopped
connections
ephemeral
the curves chromatic
darkness approaches
Ghosts hide
bumping against
limits
a turbulent evening
already
October
over here
producing
tempests
inside
the mind
must study
ourselves
at night
a child
remains
in the exchange
what did happen
to being
with others
a family of raccoons
give relief
in Riverside

Park
an attraction
where humans
melt
the majesty
of being
in place
yellow golden
aesthetic leaves
fall
an autumn night

(ER)

Seven Poems

Rae Armantrout

Count

  1

The future
is a sweetener

children have to learn
to crave.

  2

As cushy clouds
in full sun

are taken
to betoken—

Provisions

To suck dry.

To mean anything
                              by.

By itself, each breath
is a sample.

I come in, decide
what's missing.

Ions,
a concentration gradient,
and a means of transcription

just to scratch the surface.

Just to get ahead
of myself

I will need a special
proboscis.

Destinations

"You want nuggets; You got nuggets. Here!
You gonna *not* eat nuggets after I bought them.
You're gonna just eat Cheetos" she snaps

"when we're almost to our destination?"

Yes, she said "destination."

What story follows them where they're headed?

Alone at another table, a man who, like the kids,
holds a bag of Cheetos, cackles and coughs

Where does he fit in?

"Oh, I dropped my candies," he says,
in a high-pitched tone, as if imitating,
maybe mocking, a child's voice.

The Mysteries

When seen from a certain angle,
she is "mysterious and dark."
You love that about her.

Angle or distance?

*

Or you've got her number.

She's a nihilist,
an exhibitionist,

a tad precious,
pointlessly fastidious,

hermetic, cold.

*

People are obvious
until you love them.

Then they're black boxes,
deep-sixed flight recorders,
or presents that won't open.

This is why
the word why
so often sounds
like an accusation.

Dimensions

Think of

a cowboy hat
on a bobble-head
AI
atop the dash
of an electric car
in China

as depth.

Then length
is the difference

between these bare ribs
of cloud

and your white hair
somewhere

in the scrum.

Fox

To cover the material,

"trace the historic path
of a doomed train
line."

     *

To identify
              as

a cloth fox
puppet.

     *

To see your way
into
a circle of six blue flowers
beneath an indigo plateau
itself composed
of tiny blossoms –

the "hydrangea."

     *

To be named.

Some deranged water

Talking Points

Processing plant blames
living conditions.

*

Incredulity
mimics boredom.

*

Children prefer to listen
to a talking animal.

This tells us something
about the world,

but what?

*

There is thought
at work here,

but it's not traceable

to a known speaker
or agent.

*

"I'm Tiger, Tigger, Trigger,"
says the sock puppet.

Five Poems
by Forough Farrokhzad
(1934-1967)

translated by Elizabeth T. Gray, Jr.

THE CONQUEST OF THE GARDEN
fateh-ye bāq

That crow,
that flew above our heads
and into the turbulent thoughts of a wandering cloud
whose call, like a short spear, traveled the breadth of the horizon
will carry our news to the city

o   o

Everyone knows
Everyone knows
that from that cold grim window
you and I have seen the garden,
have seen the garden
and have picked the apple
from that playful branch beyond our reach

Everyone is afraid
Everyone is afraid,
but you and I, united with the lamp and the water and the mirror,
were not afraid

This is not about the flimsy linking of two names
having sex on the pages of a worn-out ledger
This is about my lucky hair
the burnt poppies of your kiss
the intimacy of our bodies, the slipperiness
and iridescence of our nakedness
like fish scales in water
This is about the silvery life of the song
that the little fountain sings at dawn

One night we asked the wild hares
in that flowing green forest
and the pearl-filled shells
in that turbulent cold-blooded sea
and the young eagles
on that solitary victorious mountain
what should be done

Everyone knows
Everyone knows
we have found the way to the cold and silent dream of the simurghs
we have found the truth in the garden
in the shy glance of a nameless flower
and eternity in an infinite moment
when two suns gazed at one another

This is not about fearful whispering in the darkness
This is about the day and open windows
and fresh breeze,
and a stove in which useless things are burning
and a land that bears fruit from a different planting
and birth, and evolving, and pride

This is about our loving hands
that have built a bridge that spans the nights
from the message of scent and light and breeze

Come to the meadow
Come to the great meadow
and call to me, from behind the breath of the silk-tree,
as the deer calls to his mate

The curtains overflow with hidden spite
and the innocent pigeons
from the heights of their white tower
look down at the earth

IN A NEVER-ENDING TWILIGHT

dar gorūbī abadī

- Day or night?
- No, O friend, it is a never-ending twilight
with two pigeons passing by on the wind
like two white coffins
and voices from far away, from that alien field,
vagrant and wavering, like the wind

○ ○

- Something must be said
Something must be said
I crave to be one with darkness
Something must be said

What a deep amnesia
An apple falls from the branch
Yellow grains of flax seeds break
in the beaks of my lovesick canaries
The fava's flower entrusts its blue tendrils to the intoxicating breeze
to escape the vague anxiety of change

And here, in me, in my head?

Ah....
There is nothing in my head except the whirling of tiny thick red particles
and my gaze
is like a lie
downcast and ashamed

- I am thinking of a moon
- I, of a word in a poem
- I am thinking of a spring
- I, of an illusion in the soil
- I, of the rich scent of a wheat field
- I, of a fairytale about bread
- I, of the innocence of games
and of that long narrow alleyway
filled with the perfume of the acacia trees
- I, of the bitter awakening after a game
and of the bewilderment after the alleyway
and of the endless emptiness after the perfume of the acacias

○ ○

- Heroics?
- Ah
The horses are old
- Love?
- It is alone and from a low window looks out
at the desert that is missing Majnun
at the pathways vaguely recalling
a delicate ankle's languid walk, its anklets

- Desires?
- They give up
at the merciless coordination of thousands of doors
- Shut?
- Yes, always shut, shut
- You will get tired

- I am thinking about a house
with the breathing of its ivies, indolent,
with its lights, like the pupil of the eye
with its pensive nights, lazy, at ease
and of a newborn with boundless smiles
like concentric circles on the water
its body plump with blood, like a cluster of grapes
- I am thinking about its collapse
and the looting by black gusts
and of a suspicious light
that at night searches into the window
and of a small grave, small as a newborn

- Work?.... Work?
- Yes, but in that big desk
lives a secret enemy
who gnaws at you very slowly
as it does the wood and the notebook
and thousands of other useless things
and in the end, you will sink in a cup of tea
like a boat in a whirlpool
and on the farthest horizon see nothing
but thick cigarette smoke
and incomprehensible lines

- A star?
- Yes, hundred, hundreds, but
all on the far side of the walled-in nights
- A bird?
- Yes, hundred, hundreds, but
all in distant memories
flapping their wings with useless pride
- I am thinking of a cry in the alleyway
- I, of a harmless mouse in the wall
that once in a while scrabbles by

o o

Something must be said

Something must be said
in the dawn, in the trembling moment
that space, like the sensation of puberty, mixes
suddenly with something vague
I want
to surrender to a rebellion
I want
to rain from that big cloud
I want
to say   No   No   No   No

- Let's go
- Something must be said
- The cup, or the bed, or loneliness, or sleep?
- Let's go….

I WILL GREET THE SUN AGAIN

be āftāb salāmī dobāreh khwaham dād

I will greet the sun again
I will greet
the stream that flowed in me
the clouds that were my long thoughts
the painful growth of the aspens in the garden
who passed with me through the dry seasons
I will greet the flock of crows
who brought me the scent of the fields at night
as a gift
I will greet my mother who lived in the mirror
and was the reflection of my old age
and greet the earth again
whose throbbing interior, with my chronic lust
I have stuffed with green seeds

I will come, I will come, I will come
with my glossy hair: rich with the scents of turned-up soil
with my eyes: experiences of dense darkness

with bushes that I have picked from the grove on the other side of the
    wall
I will come, I will come, I will come
and the threshold will be filled with love
and on the threshold
I will greet those who love again
and the girl still standing there
on the love-filled threshold

IN THE COLD STREETS OF NIGHT
dar khīābānhā-ye sard-i shab

I have no regrets
I am thinking of this surrender, this painful surrender
I kissed the cross of my fate
on the hills of my execution

o o

In the cold streets of night
couples always hesitate
to part from one another
In the cold streets of night
there is no sound but "Goodbye, Goodbye!"

I have no regrets
It's as if my heart flows on the far side of time
Life will repeat my heart
and the dandelion seed that floats on the lakes of the wind
will repeat me

Ah, do you see
how my skin stretches apart?
How the milk grows dense in the blue veins of my cold breasts?
How the blood
begins to form sinew in my patient womb?

I am you, you
and the one who loves
and the one who within herself
suddenly discovers a vague bonding
to a thousand things loaded with unknown strangeness
and I am all the fierce lust of the earth
that pulls all the waters into itself
to make all the fields fertile

Listen
to my distant voice
in the heavy mist of dawn recitations
and see me in the silence of the mirrors
how once again, with what is left of my hands
I numb the dark depth of all dreams
and I tattoo my heart, like a bloody stain
onto the innocent joys of existence

I have no regrets
Speak of me, O my lover, with the other me you will find
in the cold streets of night
with the same amorous eyes
and remember me in her sad kiss
on the sweet lines beneath your eyes

I PITY THE GARDEN

delam barā-ye bāghcheh mīsūzad

No one is thinking about the flowers
No one is thinking about the fish
No one wants
to believe that the garden is dying
that the heart of the garden has swollen under the sun
that the mind of the garden is slowly slowly
being emptied of green memories
and it's as if the garden's feelings
are a nothing rotting in isolation in the garden.

Our courtyard is lonely
Our courtyard yawns
waiting for the rain from an anonymous cloud
and our pool is empty
The tiny inexperienced stars
fall to earth from the heights of the trees
and at night the sound of coughing comes
from among the pallid windows of the fish-pond
Our courtyard is lonely.

Father says:
"It's over for me
It's over for me
I did what I had to
and finished my job"
and in his room from dawn to sunset
he reads either the *Shahnameh*
or the *History to End All Histories*
Father says to Mother:
"To hell with every fish and fowl
When I die
what difference will it make if there is a garden
or if there is not a garden?
For me, my pension is enough."

Mother's whole life
is a prayer mat spread out
on the threshold of the horrors of Hell
Mother always searches at the bottom of everything
for traces of sin's footprint
and thinks that the blasphemy of a single plant
has contaminated the garden.
Mother prays all day long
Mother is by nature a sinner
and blesses all the flowers
and blesses all the fish
and blesses herself
Mother is waiting for the arrival of the Mahdi
and His forgiveness.

My brother calls the garden a cemetery
My brother laughs at the riot of weeds
and inventories the fish corpses
that under the sick skin of the water
decompose into particles of putrefaction
My brother is addicted to philosophy
My brother thinks the cure for the garden
is the destruction of the garden
He gets drunk
and, drunk, punches everything
and tries to say
he is so afflicted and exhausted and desperate
He carries his despair with him
into the street and the bazaar
as well as his ID and calendar and handkerchief and lighter and pen
And his despair
is so small that each night
it gets lost in the crowd at the tavern.

And my sister, who was the flowers' friend
and when Mother hit her
took the simple words of her heart to their kind and silent company
and now and then treated the family of fish
to sun and sweets…
her house is on the other side of the city
She, in her artificial house
with her artificial goldfish
in the shelter of her artificial husband
and beneath the branches of her artificial apple trees
sings artificial songs
and produces real babies
Whenever she comes to see us
and the hem of her skirt is stained by the poor garden
she
bathes in eau de cologne
Whenever she comes to see us
she
is pregnant.

Our courtyard is lonely
Our courtyard is lonely
All day long
from behind the door comes the sound of chopping
and explosions
In their gardens all of our neighbors are planting
grenades and machine guns instead of flowers
All of our neighbors have covered
the tops of their tiled pools
and now the tiled pools
given no choice
are caches of hidden gunpowder
and the children of our alleyway
have filled their school backpacks with little bombs.
Our courtyard is confused.

I fear the time
that has lost its heart
I fear the idea of all these useless hands
and the appearance and strangeness of all these faces
I, like a school child
who loves her geometry lesson madly
am alone
and I think the garden could be taken to the hospital
I think…
I think…
I think…
and the heart of the garden has swollen under the sun
and the mind of the garden is slowly, slowly
being emptied of green memories.

Magnetic Adventures I-III

for John Peck

Joseph Donahue

I

Buffed by a wet breeze
from the river, the wide street
shines as, store to store, unable
to procure a pomegranate, not even
a cup of culled seeds, those
jewels of juice, you wander on,
until a bird falls silent so a further
can sing. But when the whole
forest is lost in choral song
what sole, agonized note
will guide you to the slopes
of incandescent quartz?
Planetary poles fray, twist.
Zone by zone the world shuts
down. The budding dark takes
many utterly away, leaving
a suspicion that what is now
remembered is so by no other.

Dreams return to the unknown:
the curfew of consciousness is
enforced. Clouds cluster on
the horizon. All goes dark.
You'll sleep in a large field
beside those whose affinities
with you have been closely
assessed. Your addled soul
finds its home in a fever tent.
This global death throe is
a rapture, black as the
hole below Tartarus
through which the first
rivers race out of, and
back into, existence.

II

The People's Inter-Subjectivity Party
convenes on white sands under blue water
attendants find no difficulty
breathing or moving, there,
on the ocean-floor off of
Florida, as they nominate
candidates pledged
to defends the rights of
"Created Intelligences" living
within the furthermost limit
of thought, to whom our history
is a flash of scenes, Agatha,
to Ireland, to Arctic ice,
to sculptures made from
salvaged metal depicting
a man patted down by a cop
in a festive mood once the
gun is found to be keys.
They laugh, in the warm
sun, on a bridge in Beirut

as a distraught friend says
a spirituality advanced and
quite beautiful woman, versed
in occult matters, will be at
the temple of a new religion
and, in the fervor of new truths,
might be open to romance.
It had been a long journey
even before the next message
arrived the balled-up
cellophane that might've
wrapped a muffin, that,
un-crumpled, held to the light,
showed a word completely
transparent but somehow
visible, as if within, as if
of, the shining wrap.
He took the word to be
Persian, and though that
fabled tongue of poets
and philosophers of light
was unavailable to him
given his indisputable
ignorance, the sheer beauty
of perceiving the word as if
written in light, and upon light,
as he pulled the cellophane
tight, seeing as if into it
rather than through it
He knew that it was sent,
this foreign and sacred word,
to him from a place long
thought nonexistent . . .
As for you, accept what ill
besets you. A doctor, crossing
the snow, flails in flames
in the twilight. All thought
he might ease the escalating
death rate, but it seems

that hope parts ways
with his fate, in the dark,
dropping in agony,
while, at his house, his
family sits, oblivious,
bent over a board game
where medieval bestiaries
are brought to life with
a throw of the dice.

III

Whispered to, is that right, in your
un-forgetting, told some new
hope yet to be spoken of by the
waking world? You are so
deeply healed this may be
the last of things as they were,
back when you were so broken,
now that the waking world
is fading as dreams often do,
and finally, after a long and
insufficient life, you feel
rested, you feel finally
made whole, ready, at last,
to welcome thoughts that
travelled far to find you,
in the blaze of day, as, once
only, in secret at night, where
you were shown so much,
shown lifetimes in a dream.
Such as when Picasso painted
a Mayan glyph on the back of
a cabinet door, a tangle of
arms and legs and faces,
fierce and squat, a cube of
all that is human. "Whenever
you reach for a wine glass,"

Picasso said, "let this guide
your reflections, this the
essence of existence, is,
in the eternal flow of these
shapes, all that touches upon
embodiment, all that can be said
about men and women, about
how they don't get along, but also,"
he added, as he slowly packed up
his paint and brushes, lost in wonder
at what his own mind, heart,
eyes, and fingertips, had made,
"also, those miraculous moments
when they do, when a couple
find, after much misery, that
they still enjoy each other.
Though, to be honest, I know
nothing about the Mayans,
let this glyph bless this house,
let affection flow afresh through
your flesh, and gratitude
set aglow all you gaze upon.
As you will see, in your daily
encounters with my gift,
as you wake, and life returns,
every conceivable sexual act
and yes, some that, in your
pathos and depravity, you
have yet to imagine, are
going on in the glyph, in the
whirl of limbs and torsos,
fingers, feet, teeth, tongues,
as, deep in the negative spaces,
genitals comply with what
the universe compels, every act,
as I said, and, I might add,
every beneficent feeling that
leads to, or corresponds with,
or follows, sexual acts, not

just in men and women,
either, but what is felt at every
minute throughout creation.
It may be what the Mayans
saw, it is, certainly, what I see
in seeing what the Mayans
in the maze of their glyphs,
saw, what they felt I feel
in painting in their honor,
feeling their feeling, seeing
how such feelings redeem all
pain, transfigure all suffering."

Four Days from Conspiracy

Trevor Joyce

May 23
22
it's the principle of the thing
scattering light
at an unaccustomed angle
media sources
rare earth metals
insidious at any time
and with little to lose
the nation's presses
blood from a stone
he had forgotten
though but a moment before
enjoying a hearty breakfast

May 24
24
footfall has dropped
away from the main centres
to a degree

previously unimaginable
certain instrumental numbers
bring a ready smile
anticipating healthy returns
to familiar surroundings outside
fixed or arbitrary rules
trimmed with novelty braid
failed to impress
bone eyes in a stone face

25

unencumbered assets
paved with their fallen
along rectilinear facades
so easy on the eye
they stripped away individual differences
though many birds are represented
polished by innumerable hands
our view is fogged by an
elaborately implemented
happy secretary personality
and conditions were prime
once history had occurred

26

the prophetic dream
of a museum of salt
though of a formidable sharpness
is a far cry from
carrying money and documents
in old margarine boxes
for a face-saving operation
that had some effect
in clouding apprehension
is deemed to have
tripped the lights
that made us what we are

May 25
27
five toes on each foot
annihilate their poverty
which means gauge
and modulate
the versions
of gold
ascribed to an unsuitable diet
which takes place of itself
discharging the office
often white and silky
despite considerable hardship
each our own accountant

28
he rose and walked away
picking up a signal
preferred to flannels
as if describing the future
had happened more than once
exactly as you would spinach
to understand
what is happening now
like permanent tourists
left on the table
the recovered animals
had an air of sadness

29
successive transformations
exhibiting themselves
between any two nodes or joints
whether metallic or not
instantaneous acts of mind
causing it to arch backwards
which they greatly embellish
favouring circumstances of decay
including the common rushes

putting the question
through conspicuous vacancy
can't wait to be cured

30
further analysis revealed
startling conurbations
a sofa and two chairs
unless our current knowledge
at higher densities
is used for emphasis
though not personally at risk
he climbed aboard a truck
through some recent carelessness
slotted into the barrel
with an extra running column
to use up sour milk

31
heartened by such evident
strength of feeling
tenderly codified
as childhood memories
in a domestic setting
brings about a dazed state
forcibly seizing and taking away
the sensibility of the retina
in a piece for two performers
despite the universal chill
of a most solemn judgement
so no 'furniture' survives

32
images of machine tools
sustained in wax
as anklebones of calves
make an exception in this case
of haunted meadows
still clinging to masonry

dimmed by breath
without promise of tranquility
announcing intervals
of acrid smoke
vomiting bile
over bland horizons

33
acute registers
actuated by intense humming
linger in the wound
beside splendid asphalt
in these breaking fruits
the sugars stale
with the warm colours
of evenings marked by
dismissed catalogues
in which the principal agents
preparing for their journey
keep talking out of turn

May 26
34
at the base of the tongue
several coaches in distinct
majesty lolling
where it is cold
gagged and blinded
collapsed accessories
clash with the newer
garden varieties
screaming in darkness
upset vessels of milk
otherwise unhurried
in their approach

35
it is fair to say that
little is known

concerning the action of
toxic agents
offering superior odds
combined with assurance of
sizeable damages
against the prevalence
of bad actors
putting out agreed lines
when sightseeing
offers most benefit

36
should suffocation be threatened
absent full scrutiny
of the yellow staining
focused on matters of process
such shoddy facilities
have nothing to offer
bar loss of blood
under a course of mercury
overspilling its banks
while he was observed fleeing
the eventual trial
salivating violently

37
next we come to
most possession hearings
where public adherence to
fitful treasures
sitting or kneeling on the floor
almost useless as obstacles
will have to file and serve
a vivid avarice
of the bridge members
gleaming in oblique
fire protected by gabions
could never have been

38

watching video
of her episodes among the
only people
with no memory of events
since fever broke
aggrieved and fragile
inserting himself into the plot
ardently anticipated
picture-perfect views
launched along a rope-way
the easier to extract
the enflamed gland

39

this abrupt deus ex machina
is up there with
bamboozling codgers at cards
beside the minor arteries
middle managers congregate
to flush
deliberated wisdom
of a positive variety
drowned out by alarm-calls
caught on the fly
among the optimized
and angry timber

40

the demand for clarity
will resume trading
given the distraction
nature reserves
for the ravers among us
mouthing pleasantries
he blocked his ears
in a social bubble
alongside breathless
songbirds in their luminous

nesting quarters
at the heart of the fire

41
who is it that was dreaming
he inquired
checking for trapped ideas
ambition slipped
from one face to another
eager to sell the project
teaches you how to
respond in difficult situations
with consciousness fighting
an unavailing battle
hoping to reunite it
with its loving owner

42
zeal for obscurity
is valued in the drone
as the entire edifice
shakes apart
in localized tremors
oscillating amusingly
the heads of zoo exhibits
nod in unison
with provocative architecture
in an occupation level
geared for failure
under rule of law

Extinction diaries

Nancy Gaffield

The Bramble Cay Melomys

At the beginning was the Bramble Cay Melomys
                                    a little brown rat
who scrambled on the rocky outcrop on an island of sand
                                    fringed by coral gardens
                                    & ribbon reefs
rich with algae, trumpet & unicorn fish
                                    the first to die
of climate change not so long ago, no not long

like a quiet crab or the tentacle blooms of a sea anemone
                                    ghost gear
                                    haunts the reef
the women come each morning to weave it into baskets
& so the world divides into resource and waste

The Nightcap Oak

Throughout the summer, drought and high temperatures. Fine dust
winnowing from the vast plains the colour of dried blood.
Shifting and undulating tree vocalisations, rumours of fire
and flight. Root-to-root alerts fizzed through the wood-wide
fungi. Air bubbles clotting the xylem. No more water.

The firefighters cried when they heard the screams of the animals
they could not save—koalas, wallabies, wombats and
kangaroos. An estimated one billion died—the Albert's
Lyre Bird, the Rufus Scrub Bird, the Log Runner, the Tree
Creeper, the Cat Bird. All the birdsong in the world goes
back to them.

Today there is no song. The ghostly trunks of the nightcap oaks
abrade the clouds, scratching out their stories of Gondwana-
-uninterrupted continent of beetles, spiders, snakes and ants,
the scent of vegetation, soil, plants and wood rotting down,
the musky smell of petrichor minutes before the rains came.

Arctic Sea Ice

                          once abundant lichen, shrubs and sedge
the tundra slumps to mud
                    the Arctic sea ice is all but gone
                    to stream flows
musk oxen and reindeer look on as the rivers fill with
                    petroleum waste
a world of brackish lakes where beluga swim

                          like the orcas, the icebergs trail their dying
          calves
glaciers ride their own melting
                    the sea ice whistles and hums

ice remembers &
the colour of its memory
is blue

Transuranic Waste

They made up their minds to build a waste isolation plant [WIPP]
in the desert. All the assurances from the mouths of
presidents gathered thick as scales on the pangolin. The
time came to bury the transuranic waste [TRU]. They chose
the site in the shrubland southeast of Carlsbad. They chose
it because of the salt a half-mile underground. They chose
it because it is the largest desert in North America, even
though 130 species of mammals and 3000 species of plants
live there.

Time passed, presidents died and their assurances were buried
with them like their wedding rings. They needed to warn
people. People needed to know not to disturb the sema
[divine omen: grave]. They called on the experts: geologists,
biologists, astronomers. They called on architects,
anthropologists, historians and linguists. They asked them
to devise an aggressive structure to deter for ten millennia.
They searched for a signifier to outlast the half-life of waste,
the half-life of language.

Then came the engineers, the bosses and the politicians to break
the ground. Dust billowed from the shovels of the men in
hard hats. Twenty years passed. The miners carved their
names in the ancient salt. The bosses and the professors
of salt, choking on the dust of dead languages, disappeared
into the gypsum dunes.

TRU is buried in the desert of New Mexico. The miners dream
of their names mummified in salt a half mile underground.
The experts could find no words to warn future generations
for what is buried there.

Steller's Sea Cow

                                    in the shallows
                          ebb and flow
                          kelp ribbons
wave with the tides   shoals of sea urchins, in-
                          dispensable
to sea otters in the frigid Arctic waters
                                    hummocks fringe the coast
                          the eye distorts the contour
                          of ice floes
                          the cruellest wind
Steller's ship, the St. Peter, ran aground and broke apart
                          stranding Steller and some other men
                          mud
                          moss
                          whalebone
and there trawling in the sands   a black shape with skin like bark
                          the sea cow
                          he named
'a man in a boat can move among them without danger
                          select the one
                          he desires'
when they came to cut up her body, her mate was still waiting
                          'her milk
                          is very rich and sweet
                          the breasts
                          when boiled
a little harder than beef with the odour of game but mild'
                                    Steller died in the Arctic
and all that remains of his creatures are the words he gave them
                          'placid'
                          'loyal'
                          'delicious'

The Albama Pigtoe Mussel

                                                    what was there to be seen
slow-moving, brackish water ripe with
                              soughs
                              oxbows
                                                      bayous of cypress-gum
bottomland forests and submerged grass beds
                              the wail
                              of the loon
                                        sometimes I feel like I'm
                                        almost done
                                        a long long way from home

the Alabama Pigtoe Mussel, brown, non-
                              descript
                              except for
                              concentric circles
to count one hundred was not unusual   each circle
                              a year

mussels are filter-feeders, purifying the river but also ingesting toxic
pollution
                              industrial waste in the gravel
                              riffles
                              of the streams
Extinct Species #37

                                      what is seen
                              the paper mill
                              the oil storage tanks
                              an industrial railroad

at Africa-town the people arrived on the schooner Clotilda in 1860
                              illegal cargo
the people were unloaded & dispersed
                              the ship scuttled
                              & burned
at Africatown the people & the molluscs are one
                              & the truth travels on the far-carrying
                              cry of the loon

The Yangtze River Dolphin

                     & yet listen

           to the water

           this was the day

when there were hundreds of combinations of clicks and whistles,

           the river

           brimming with the sounds of

sonar so finely tuned that they could locate each

           other &

           even

           individual fish

confident in their time, the slow passing of

           twenty million years

the river ran free, till one day a man appeared who said: 'humans

           must conquer nature'

           & the baiji found themselves

           in a darker

           louder

           world

ships dragging lines of hooks snagging & slashing

           the tender skin

           of their young

& the river seethed with foam laden with heavy metals and sewage

           O

           River of Death

& a sequence of lakes & power stations, sedimentation turning the

           water

           turgid

           with plastic

carried by the river to the sea. In fifty years the baiji were gone

           rock

           water

           flesh

           soil

we are all the river, we are all downstream, and nothing

           exists but

           love

Miss Waldron's Red Colobus

you thought that the old growth forests would be growing forever
African mahogany & wawa trees, but 'if you come to look
                              for trees in this forest then forget it
                              because we have cut them all'

they deserved to have their own name, not this one—
                              Miss Waldron's Red Colobus
                              like someone's
                              lapdog
colobus from the Greek word for docked, or amputated, thumb-
                              less
no milk of human kindness for them, the world wants
                              more & more
bauxite for beverage cans & cars, cobalt for batteries & planes
                              gold
                              & chocolate

these primates will not come back, their forests are gone
                              you'll not hear
their shrieks & chattering in the high canopy
                              only the ground's un-
                              interrupted drone
                              of extraction

The White-Tailed Eagle

                              once found in wetlands
                              the Norfolk Broads
& peat bogs
                              the Somerset Levels
the sea eagle ranged the wrong side of history, out of place
                              vermin
                              dead birds flying
they fished the lakes
                              dry
                              they ate

              greedily
the church wardens paid for their killing
              they fully disappeared

one day long after, three pairs were released
              their eight-foot wings
              out of scale with the British
              countryside

look how their golden eyes read you, standing here in the offshore
              wind where the river pulses
she finds her mate, they lock claws mid-air
              cartwheel to earth
loosening only a few feet from the ground &
              open out for the sea
listen how they master discourse
              gri-gri-gri
              krau-krau-krau-krau
haunting the fragile line between
              enough
              & not

Plastic World

Plastic carrier bags were introduced into the supermarkets in the
        1980s, and now a trillion are produced each year. I cannot
        comprehend a trillion. Is it one thousand times one billion, or
        one million times one billion?
I was trying to think about this incomprehensible figure when I read
        about a hot blob in the Pacific Ocean which has killed a
        million murres. Murres, or common guillemot, are large auks.
        The blob stems from a years-long heatwave. This heat led
        to a vast bloom of algae, harmful to sea lions, puffins and
        baleen whales. The birds probably died of starvation.
Not one death, but many. A dead zone, a wingbone.

In some areas of the Mediterranean there is more plastic than
        plankton. Both plant and animal, plankton are drifters. They

consume carbon dioxide and release oxygen. I am
a drifter too but I consume oxygen and produce carbon
dioxide. The plankton feed the creatures of the sea; I/we eat
them. The average person ingests 5 grams of plastic every
week. That is the equivalent of a credit card.

In Manilla, Smokey Mountain is the world's largest litter dumpsite
where 30,000 people comb through the trash for items to
sell. Layer after layer of plastic bags, wood, metal, bottles,
iron, fabrics, tires and more plastic bags. Chicken discarded
from a restaurant is cleaned, wrapped in fresh plastic bags
and re-sold for 20 pesos. A scavenger gets paid 16 pesos
for plastics, one peso per kilo of broken glass, and 16 pesos
for metals. On a good day, they will make $11.

The lifespan of a plastic bag is approximately 12 minutes. Each
plastic bag takes between 500-1000 years to break down.
The Swedish inventor thought they would save the planet
from trees being destroyed to make paper bags.

Five Poems

Zoë Skoulding

A Maritime Vocabulary

what travessia/trip/travesia/trajet
                              traverses
        the wreck/naufragio/
naufragio/naufrage

of language underwater
        glimpsed through bones and rafters

whose is this zone/zona/zone/zona
        where I am passenger and cargo

and the anchor is a
        weight/peso/peso/poids
                and nothing floats freely

not even the cargo of words
        while the names of the dead
                are still sinking

this self/mesmo/mismo/soi
        all at sea/mar/mar/mer
no more than a murmur

in the hold/porão/bodega/cale

there may be dates dental instruments
       detergent
            drafting paper dyestuff

or solvents spark plugs spectacles
           staplers sunflower seeds

that is to say
       it's a mixed vessel/navio mixto/
navío mixto/navire mixte
         carrying only names

say vessel that is my speech
say mouth
      boca/width/anchura/largeur
           say open sea

Stellar Bearing Pro Forma

I am south of lyre
I am north of scorpion
I am east of eagle
I am some way west of swan

       this is my angle of tilt
          how's yours

balancear de una borda a otra   to roll
    to a tipping point

       reach to the brightest star
isolated and little-seen

noting the altered positions

still   visible

trazar un rumbo   to trace a route
here we go rumbling on

what lies
                                    in the water
a sea shaken to its depths

                        run your finger
up the left-hand edge

                identify as/with
                                constellations
in the second you speak
                                a second enters
            in the pull and reach
            of daily rotation

suppose that
                        lies roughly in line with

            a hand searches air

                light falls
                    behind a minute

a rusting winch
            a chain dragged over rocks

Voyage

close by is a silver branch
etched with frost I couldn't
tell you where the twigs end
and the white flowers begin

bearing a kind of glitter
baring the edge of blue
pebbles churn underwater
mutating colours of the sea

in yesterday's weather cloud
glistens in ridges of sand
turning on a mussel shell
there in the mist behind the sky

dolphins and porpoises leap
in rings around the island birds
call to the hours there is music
somewhere playing silently

a storm is passing through
eyes far off in the distance
I can't turn into a picture
with receding perspective

there were two blackbirds on the
branch and a single robin now
the robin is gone and a
single blackbird is waiting

If anyone asks

if anyone asks who you are   say you are nobody   and no
body is washed up   on the shores of this poem   and nobody can
sing when everything   conspires to shut you up and the
song doesn't   start anywhere or ever finish   the frame collapses
and this love   won't stay out of that one   flashed up on a screen
too fast   to read the name   filmed with voice-overs or washed
    away   sailing the wine-blue   to peoples of alien speech
your words are like the words of what changes in the blood
    eating the flowers made me forget the way home   in a
structure that was   just a slow process this was   the music   my
mind moved along the info stream assimilating   which is not to
say becoming similar   the thread of a life takes form   in an eye
travelling down   for surely your words are like an octopus
    dragged with pebbles in its suckers   like the wash of the great
sea   like an island on the edge of an island   like seafall sucked
over stones   in the grip of the sea   I forgot my own name   an
assemblage of cells   here the eyes   there the oiled skin   and
grey-eyed Athene went away with the likeness of a vulture   for
the dead are very close   to the edge of the world   translucent
fish and islands in luminous water   in the wake of the ship
interrupting itself   where a passport is a hollow vessel   this face
is like your face   you pass with biometric data   where all the eyes
had turned into a single eye   and the shutters go down   you
arrive in the likeness of a gannet   and the shutters shut against
you   and who put out the giant eye   it was nobody my name is
nobody   in the likeness of an owl   to allow the bearer to pass
freely   without let or hindrance   in the name of every which
way wind   as when an octopus is dragged from its shelter   so
the rocks tore at his skin   so the storm that was in my heart
    raged as weather systems whorled like fingerprints   what word
escapes your teeth's barrier   when you speak of them coming out
of the sea   encrusted with salt   what it means to be leaving
in the likeness of a cormorant   so many leaving in the likeness
of a seagull   so many leaving in the likeness of a heron   so
many leaving in the likeness of an egret   so who are you   do
you remember our bed made of a still-rooted olive   do you
remember our bed planed with a brazen adze   a place without

right of seizure   skin bathed clean of salt and rubbed with oil
such assistance and protection as necessary   the singer was blind
and he was nobody   they were struggling up the sides of the
ship   with ropes and ladders   their hands and feet were cut and
slipping   these feet are like your feet   my heart was a storm in
me as I went   and the journeying ways were darkened   this
face is like your face and these hands are like your hands

A Presentation on the Current Direction of Travel

we are where we are we are where we are we are where
we are we are where we are we are where we are we are
where we are we are where we are we are where we are
we are where we are we are where we are we are where
we are we are where we are we are where we are we are
where we are we are where we are we are where we are
we are where we are we are where we are we are where
we are we are where we are we are where we are we are
where we are we are where we are we are where we are
we are where we are we are where we are we are where
we are we are where we are we are where we are we are
where we are we are where we are we are where we are
we are where we are we are where we are we are where
we are we are where we are we are where we are we are

Six Poems

Elizabeth T. Gray, Jr.

How to Live at the Front: The Listening Post
July 1917

The listening post will be well away from the noise of your lines
in a shell crater or sap run out a little way into "No Man's Land."

The object is to give quick warning of hostile patrols,
raids, and worse still, poison gas.
Information can be gleaned about movement in enemy trenches,
for example, whether troops are being relieved or not.

You must listen carefully.
If an arrow sounds as if it is wrapped in silk
it is a divination arrow. Gas canisters clank
in a certain way when carried.
Gas emission can be heard.

You will find it difficult not to imagine quite a lot.

Your officers will want to know a great deal

about all sorts of little things. Your information
must not be imaginary. It must be as accurate as possible:
Is there a cairn?
Was the hand drum of wood or bone?

Little bits of information put together
make something for the staff people to work on.
The result of your work will appear in reports
issued to men of your Army Corps.

Carry with you nothing of interest to the enemy.
He will try, if possible, to take you alive.
It will depend on the amount of barbed wire around you.

Facing No Man's Land

Of the many things she said to me there are two
of which I'm certain:

There are many vermilion terraces
each with its own light and very fearful brilliance.

and

Any kind of break in the line
must be used sparingly.

About Time
7th Infantry Brigade, 3rd Canadian Division, Belgian Flanders
28 October 1917

The Signaling officer will take a synchronized watch to Brigade Signal
Office at 9.15 a.m. and 6.15 p.m. daily to check the time.

Reliable watches must be used for synchronization and they must be
set so that the second hand and minute hand agree.

An hour hand is of no importance. Watches missing a second hand must not be used.

In synchronizing watches the exact error of the watch should be noted and written down.

No attempt should be made to set the watch to the exact correct time. The exact correct time is of no importance.

What matters is that each of us, taking into account our exact individual error, will be in the same time.

Wherever that occurs we will know when we are.

From *The Twenty-Five Ways of Averting Armies*, Appendix F: The Sequenced Classification of Means for Averting a Whole Regiment

Repelling with tactical and protective obstacles.

Repelling through giving the appearance of a general offensive on the whole battle front by simultaneous attacks on the enemy's flanks in order to pin down his reserves and force him to disperse his artillery fire.

Repelling through controlling the elements.

Repelling by breaking up the enemy's attack formation, restricting his power to maneuver, forcing his troops into positions in which they are more easily dealt with by fire, particularly machine gun fire.

By a relentless advance as far as possible without a pause.

Repelling by crumpling a paper effigy of a general.

Through inundations, a sunken obstacle, French wire, belts of concertina, a double apron fence or simple four-strand fence of spider wire.

By subduing *shidaks* and *sadaks* and other ground demons in order to make them paralyze troops and cut off their route.

With white mustard seed.

By suppressing hostile fire over the area to be crossed by the attacking infantry long enough to enable assaulting troops to reach the cover of the enemy's defenses.

With magical substances in water (*chu la rdzas kyis ngar blud de zlog pa*), with *yé* materials, *mdos* rituals, burnt offerings, and magical *torma* weapons.

By demanding in all ranks dash and gallantry of a very high order, down to the lowest grades, a quick perception, rapid decision-making, and intelligent initiative.

Repelling by means of the utmost steadfastness and devotion.

At Zero Hour
Pilkem Ridge, Belgian Flanders
31 July 1917

The body melts into light within a vast translucence.

I think this means we are all together in some place.

A flare breaks the night as past or reminiscence.

Because storm cells roll over us so fast we experience this weather in one piece, as if we are a magnificent cape of feathers seen from space.

Gaps in the wire widen until they touch one another.

The Dream About the Lady in the Café in the Grote Market
Ypres, 1928

When she leaves he and I don't know what to do, we are at a loss,
he at the table at the center of the damaged city in a clearing of light
among mists and I here at my desk in this moment of where has she
gone what will he do does he see who she is will he follow her.

As the sound of her heels fades on the paving stones the light begins
to contract.

Every street looks equally empty to him, no matter where he runs
looking for her everywhere is a maze in progress, hedges of khaki
scaffolding between small piles of what had been a house promising
a precise replica of what is no longer there.

Because I stand up and step away from his time and his panic I can
see her clearly from here:

> Her body is the white of a conch shell
> with one face and two hands.
> Her hair flows down her back.
> Her left hand supports a silver bell at her hip.
> The right plays a golden drum in the sky.

NOTES TO THE POEMS

"How to Live at the Front" draws on Hector Macquarrie, *How to Live
at the Front: Tips for American Soldiers.* (Philadelphia and London:
J. B. Lippincott, 1917. 141-144)

"Facing No Man's Land" draws on *Machik's Complete Explanation:
Clarifying the Meaning of Chöd*, translated by Sarah Harding (Ithaca,
New York, and Boulder, Colorado: Tsadra Foundation, Snow Lion
Publications, 2003, 239); and from Thomas Lux on the line in *A
Broken Thing: Poets on the Line* (Iowa City, Iowa: University of Iowa
Press, 2011, 155-156).

"About Time" draws on "Instructions for the Offensive No. 2: Synchronization of Watches." Unit War Diary, Princess Patricia's Canadian Light Infantry, for 28 October 1917. Narrative of Operations, Appendix B.
http://data2.collectionscanada.ca/e/e043/e001072740.jpg

"From the Twenty-Five Ways of Averting Armies" draws on James Gentry, "Representations of Efficacy: The Ritual Expulsion of Mongol Armies in the Consolidation and Expansion of the Tsang (Gtsang) Dynasty" quoting text transmitted to Sodokpa by Zhigpo Lingpa, revealed to him in 1544 at Eagle Nest Rock, in *Tibetan Ritual*, José Ignacio Cabezón, Ed. (New York: Oxford University Press, 2010, 136-137); from *The Official History of the Great War: Military Operations: France & Belgium 1917. Vol. II.* (London: Her Majesty's Stationery Office, 1948, 349, 355, 382); from *Manual of Field Works (All Arms) 1921 (Provisional)* (London: His Majesty's Stationery Office, 1921, 47-49, 57); and from *British Trench Warfare 1917-1918: A Reference Manual.* (General Staff, War Office, London: The Imperial War Museum and Nashville, Tennessee: The Battery Press, 1997, 8-12).

"At Zero-Hour" draws from "Giving the Body in Charity to Beings of the Six Realms," *Machik's Complete Explanation: Clarifying the Meaning of Chöd*, translated by Sarah Harding (Ithaca, New York, and Boulder, Colorado: Tsadra Foundation, Snow Lion Publications,167).

"The Dream About the Lady in the Café at the Grote Markt in Ypres, 1928" draws on Karma Chakme, *Rgyun khyer lus sbyin bsdud pa*, "Abridged Charity of the Body for Daily Practice," in *Machik's Complete Explanation: Clarifying the Meaning of Chöd*, translated by Sarah Harding (Ithaca, New York, and Boulder, Colorado: Tsadra Foundation, Snow Lion Publications, 33, 346).

Five Poems

Danielle Hooke Goodbody

Now Leave the House

Moonlight moonlight moonlight. Galahad,
what does it mean to find? There isn't the time
to explore such economics & what all
could be called sacrifice. What all of this
or that world was sacrificed. The hills the hills

The hills. Or any world & what of it was sacrificed,
revealing itself in scorched grass to remain
in the memory of a coastal winter.
How it would be nice to say a small boat left
this beach, and fine, much much more than fine
to say it was just a dream or the dream of a song.

Have control over this evening, someone says
to themselves. Have control over yourself in this
evening, someone says. A dream comes, if you find
the proper temperatures. Now leave the house
before these rooms are let out, the knife closed

in a pocket, its certain brass, its rosewood scales.

> No one can control themselves
> on an evening like this—
> The spiraling leaves,
> no need for a shield

Myths of the White Oak

This my exuberant white oak & these the boards covering my coracle

    on this my setting out

These the longest arms in the landscape

    asking for lightning, coaxing wrath from

                gods of thunder

This my search for the solid wood of

        my decades

On the shore as I am, I try to make a prayer into a work

    song, the shore as I have found it ghosts a shanty

    & which prayer is not a work song?

I am trying to think straight upwards

    while the oak roots do the real work

    of speech throughout the understory

Prince of Hares says to the oak, *What are you for?*

& the oak, in exhaustion, *I am the arrows*

which fell true enemies, rest for the war-tired back

Various homes claim a single tree. My god, if you find yourself

at home   [stay at home

My tongue

      is all

My eyes

      are all   of rough bark

      [Let it be said of me that I have gone

Autogeography

Must never dwell. This place rolls us away
& sweeps us back. My youth was a bank? A vault
of green? I stole away. My god, there were coyotes
in the small stretch of woods. Remember they never
howled or came after the dogs. Nothing left to say about
standing silently in the street. Someone is being spoken to sleep
      & it isn't me.

I am home. I am in a house on a cliff
& I am laughing with you & the wind tripping
through the windows. I can no longer muster a fear
of anything under the water. There are dogfish on the beach
every day, eyes closed like rest. A single dogfish on the beach
every day. A four-count of vodka. Someone is coming home from
work
      & it isn't me.

This is another journey down
through the layers of temperature—
it is not simply winter. I am willing to settle in
here. After all, I have watched & now on the air

the taste of the dripping bells of action. A shuttered
foundry
                      & I was never at home.

                      What a quick dim afternoon we will spend here

Wheel Prayer

I suppose I
stopped long ago,
but still the river goes
on. Who are any of us now
to the great machinery? Just palms

against ordained direction. Digging
nails into morning's sharp turn,
waking into a day of bored
rubber, the river better
off without us

Wednesday Cloak

wears somebody above the bright colours
of the service industries. The fractal imagery
of speech, bacterial bright orange

        slips of plastic
                now

The cloak came down after the humidity
bored itself & communication
away

        Cloud—
all cloud this day, this pilgrim city
& the kidnapped coast— the kidnapped
from the coast, settled in the whole sky

Domed in the postdrome coming back round
to the prodrome, breaking the bright colours
of a poisoned productivity

                    Bones
are such sunshine someone says. All up there together
the sparrows & gulls
                              dodging what we
                              know of
                              the dusklands

This isn't difficult.
Where are you whose plummeting rips the cloth
of homeache? Where, you winged? The drop
& purr, sleeping now on the sandbar.
                    Does it disturb   ?
                    Does it sharpen   ?

Cloud funneled itself right down into dagger
point & I never
existed in any industry
at all

Reading Jack Spicer

Joel Chace

Skinny paper slips

months ago stuffed, forgotten,

now loosen from the book's

center, flutter across

a blue comforter.

In green: *to get good, this*

glow, restaurant, weapon,

the latch, nowhere. In red:

I'm X, means that. In

yellow: *shore, loop,*

listen like hell.

Scattered over blue.

***

I'm X means that I

listen like hell:_____*proposed new figures*

for the height of Lucifer,

triangulated from the circumference

of the earth, the height of the giants

and the distance of Hell's lowest circles.

on

the yellow shore where

green birds step and breezes

bring tears; in any

restaurant where whisperings

are a red wind; in traffic

loops, radio static _____*The complex spectrum with rising and*

falling tones is very similar

to Earth's auroral emissions.

a blue circulation.

I listen like

hell to get good again.

***

This glow _____*An electron moving in a medium*

does radiate light even if it is

moving uniformly provided

that its velocity is greater than the

velocity of light in the medium.

from the red

planet. A radio

plays in a furnished, latched

room. Listen. If you don't

like hell, _____*I think that you'll never enter*

Bohemia...but for poetry -- to

see the windows and maybe blast a few

yourself through the rocks of hell. I'll be

there waiting for you, my arms open.

    move. Somewhere. Nowhere.

Just take a weapon along.

      ***

When any center _____*A box-and-whisker*

plot provides a visual

way of understanding both

the range and the middle.

    scatters,

colors switch: red with

yellow; blue with green. Latches

begin to click; newspaper

ink rewinds; comforters

flutter -- X _____*When while*

becomes

infinite --

while(y<10)

  x=x+1:

end

No

end.

-- to a

new job; forgotten

others head to the shore

by all necessary means.

                                    ***

That restaurant gives

as good as it takes. Across

the highway a farmer

walks among his cows. He's

proud they're skinny, not stuffed; in

truth, he sees their gauntness _____...*white snow and leafless trees, and a*

winding track; but close to the sledge

were three dark wasted animals...

as a weapon. Once

he latches his barn doors,

the beasts inside start

a green glow. _____*For the delicate task of applying*

the paint to the tiny dials, the women were

instructed to point the brushes with

their lips. They became known as Radium Girls.

          Basking in it,

yonder, the diners smile.

                                    ***

Loop-d-loop; lie-d-lie. Months

later, still no knowledge, _____*...language is...a knowing, an event...*

as words are important to hold on to

whatever it is that composes us.

nor nowhere, nor all the

bluebooks in the world. Getting

good means finding that island,

squatting near the green

sea, deciphering

octopus _____*...three hearts*

and blue blood...

       ink.

Loop-d-loop; lie-d-lie.

A comfort: slip of the tongue.

Seeds

You'll probably want to see

this, the archive of every

unsaid sentence. *In night's*

icy font: seed-hoe

with tattered diploma nailed

to its handle; daily

bread; kitchen table and

restless hands; already

drying, dying tongues;

the tiniest

circles ever. That could

be one. This might be

another -- *Here comes*

a copper to bop off

your head. Or, *How can*

a preview hurt?

***

So someone told the

faster-than-the-speed- of-light

joke, while restless regulars

study their cards, never

guessing what's buried right

beneath. Talk about

a preview. _____*With practice, it should be possible*

to detect patterns or peaks which might

even suggest the nature and potential

date, time and place of a disaster.

　　　　　The upshot

being that it arrived before

getting there. Ass's jawbone,

ancient giant curled into

a seed, _____*They belonged to the Judean Date Palm species,*

which had been a staple crop for thousands of years

but became extinct by 500AD after

the Romans wiped them out in an

attempt to cripple the Jewish economy.

circle of torn-out

hair, assbone of a

fool, half a heart.

***

Take physics, pomp. And having

in earliest sections

referenced the over-arching

title does not entail

continuance or even

previews. _____*It would be wrong for me to say that I was not*

frightened by a prediction of this nature.

I intend keeping a diary from now on and to

record my reactions to this on a daily

basis. I suppose anybody who plays about

with precognition in this way to some extent

sticks his neck out and must accept what he gets.

Dust, glows,

rushings, other

wonders. Widening

sanctuaries _____*No longer could they take*

refuge behind the temple walls.

become

possible. One could even

speak about pieces of air.

***

A voice grows louder

in the street. A window in

the third story shoots up. As

those tongues _____*The new brain scans contrasted*

sharply with images taken of

other spiritually inspired

mental states like meditation.

           in the street

grow louder, a window

shoots up three stories

above. When they tire

of learning, they say so. Which,

supposedly, is

good. Which? good? Demarcating

alleluias from

rapture, the sundial, _____*It was found on the floor of a*

workman's hut in the Valley of the Kings.

           in her

garden, the sundial

demarcates alleluias

from raptures.

So. So. Tired.

                ***

More often lately, the bus

overshoots their stop. Line

of tiny circles along

the road's shoulder. The familiar

hoe leaning against its tree,

sundial, _____*In time, Egyptians made them*

portable, smaller

versions of the obelisks.

            ground ivy. Someone has

bequeathed them that house, which never

comes closer for all their trudging.

In the story, a heart breaking _____*The normal organ appears as if it has*

literally been broken and the left

ventricle stretches out to form

a narrow neck-shaped section.

ceremony at the end.

                              ***

Fitting in easier next time,

right? Jagged chunks of classroom

buildings, archives, _____*Native diggers sold*

piecemeal what they found there.

                    explode over

the campus lawns, but no one

really to blame. Can't be too much

to ask: gliding a half-inch

above hallowed pathways; ink

already drying on the

diploma. Sanctuary _____*That scene with Jaweh walking*

in the cool of the garden.

soon

to shrink in the rearview

mirror for the final time.

***

In the instructors' parlor,

students, restless. One way to

dig up trouble but avoid

police. They do keep on

trying though they think of it as

a living room and of themselves

as a half-circle of tiny

easels. Like windows shooting

up, words rise -- rupture,

rapture? air barrage,

arbitrage? _____$?E(R) \; I? = E(R)z \; ?+ (E(I) \; ? \; E(R)z?) \times ?n$

         Those teachers seem

intimate yet rather

pruney as though submerged too

long in the font. _____*Nobody knows why it had been*

                                           covered and put in this place and

                                           never written about

                                           in any historical book.

         One draws

the students while the other

draws out of them

such as may be cleaned.

***

To practice arbitrage _____*So, there is no doubt that this, in theory,*

is something that can be a great benefit

to the investors as well as the traders.

by

the river bank. Later he stood

and rose up on a

dictionary that covered

a stunned bat. So use that word

in a sentence. Seizing the day,

or rather the carp, _____*If the carp successfully makes the jump*

over the mythical Gate, it

transforms into a powerful dragon.

only

long enough to unhook and

release it. Now that word

has been used in this sentence.

***

Burst pod: dark seeds _____*They grew but did not at all look*

like the picture she sent. We were

completely devastated.

flecking

a cloudy white that clings to tufts

of fur on the forest floor. So.

Another mystery

born. Grows. Summon the

unusual testifiers.

All quite enough to make one

wail. Enough to shake

one's heart. Enough to split a

heart in two, _____*Takotsubo Cardiomyopathy is*

the medical term.

        then

break each half.

                ***

They did whatever it took

to get out of weeding. Angling for carp, _____*It used to be said that only seventy*

could make the climb in any year. When the first

succeeded, then the rains would begin to fall.

      much cooler business.

Later, under duress, they

testified that their sloth had been

weaponized. Strange, rising word.

                ***

Archivist _____*Most of the time we cannot tell whether*

we are dealing with an archival aggregate or a

collection of trash, the equivalent

of a modern waste-paper basket

     of licenses, she

frequently observed that

a cleaver could cleave a carp _____*I shall transcend the estate of ordinary*

fish and achieve a place among the order of

sacred dragons. I shall rid myself forever

of the terrible suffering to which

my race is heir, expunge every trace

of our shame and humiliation.

but then could not cleave it. Fatty

Arbuckle _____*At some point, Arbuckle and Rappe ended*

up together in a bedroom, from where,

minutes later, her screams were heard.

might very well

have kept his own scrapbook. That was

another fish flopping and

drying in the dirt. Dead

people, and broken things.

***

When he offers to eat a

crocodile, it's like, O.K.,

we get it; he really does

love her. What Gertrude did know,

and when she did know it. So

many tongues _____*Based on a recent study of nearly*

1,000 evangelicals,

researchers have identified at least

two forms of the practice, one ecstatic and

frenzied, the other subdued and nearly silent.

lolling in

the promise-crammed air. And what, at

the end, they both did

finally know. And even

Arbuckle, _____*Acquittal is not enough*

for Roscoe Arbuckle.

      for that

matter. Dead and broken, all.

         ***

Redeeming avocations:

digging up jawbones, grabbing

tapestries of air. Breath in a

wide sanctuary, _____*Silence isn't the*

absence of something but

the presence of everything.

      hair rings,

fonts, _____*They were astonished*

to find the one

so long sought-after hidden

inside another.

    crocodile necklaces,

sundial bracelets. Judges

sustain secrets and say, Quashed.

Testimony becomes them.

         ***

JOEL CHACE | 161

Freshly weeded, seeded

lawns, one beyond the other

until they make tiny

circles. Freshly cleaved carp

ready in the kingdom's

freezers. All regulars

released, permitted raptures

and alleluias, then

rounded back up once the

sundial's first shadow falls. Less

bequest than testament.

Less tongue itself than words.

("Reading Jack Spicer" is a consequence of my reading Jack Spicer, specifically his seminal collection My Vocabulary Did This to Me, a book that I've read, returned to, and reread over decades. My most recent encounter began months ago, in the long-long-time-ago, pre-covid days. When I opened the text, ten to twelve thin, short strips of paper fluttered down into my lap. Right away, I recognized them as remnants from a visual poetry project completed years earlier. Why they'd ended up in that book, I've no recollection.   However, as I looked over the single words and phrases printed in tiny fonts of different colors -- the words and colors that are included in the first section of my poem -- it seemed strangely yet wonderfully appropriate that those messages had been delivered to me as if from Jack's Martians. I couldn't possibly refuse them.

The italicized, right hand commentary riffing off the key seed words is a method I'd just started to employ in previous writings. It's a procedure that fell into my head, also serendipitously.)

3 pages from House-girl

Dorothy Lehane

on the third day my brothers skin the divining rod
but she sneaks the lace-bug inside

lace-bark-bugs traveling up her arms
& under her bandages. the itch starts

reliable as hunger
every girl here suffers the same fate

washes out her mouth with oil
it is a slow dance & after

she can pronounce the alphabet perfectly
announces a game of hunt & rescue

this is a game for lovers
who aren't allowed to touch

forfeiting is the rescue
but the hunt hangs in the air

as if both a gesture & warning
house girl: affectionate but listless

on the fourth day her brothers
take her to the reservoir

the water resists
she feels the tension in the Schlag-ruthe

my sisters promise to rattle the energy out
with fire & warm dances

leaping up. sage & bay leaves
wrap my thoughts with string

these are the old ways
they meet her in the sweet-grass

fan her with ash from a clay pot
inrush to the inside of words

on the fifth day they baptize me with parasites
& mistle-thrush *in case she dies before we wake*

on the sixth day they smoke out each limb
mama, you gave her bad breast milk

so we bathed her again & again on the lawn
mama, we hear the bird you put in her stomach

on the seventh day the wound of the wings
across her hips: the world beginning to happen

on the eighth day we placed clothes
other people had worn across her stomach

tried to coax the bird out. she kept still
but even in stillness the body rises up

to comfort itself. under the crab apple tree,
she falls into fits. always wearing white

& drinking black juices. do words help recovery
do words ever help

the syntax of recovery is a broken mechanism
the condition of thinly scattering

dowsing occurs from the core
takes the shape of childish mottos

by the ninth day she was living inside the bird
call up your brothers dilly dilly set them to hunt

into which they poured new medicines
you shall be buried dilly dilly under the tap

lend me your ear: the taste of lengthy grief
knitted into tiny herbs. except we are double loathed

for caterwauling. full of baseness & idolatry
one problem slips into the next

we call it quantum collapsing.
the wave function is hope. also uncountable

& this is the sound we make when we discard
our bodies & absorb material spaces.

from Nature:
Chapter VI, Idealism

Norman Fischer

Thus in all these ways Nature schools us.
And we might ask: Is this the point of Nature?
Does Nature exist in herself or is she a mere figment of human
mentality? For surely what we sense of Nature is sensed and
thought in us.
How can we be sure there is something outside our minds or if so
what it is. Man and woman, sun and moon, house and trade: I can't
know for certain whether any of it exists beyond my knowing — and
what is the meaning of this question? And what difference would
it make whether Orion is really up there in the sky or just God's
painting of scenery in my brain? Who knows whether the feeling of
Wholeness and Oneness is in me from out there or merely my own
delusion, whether land and sea, star and cloud, deep yawning into
deep, galaxy beyond galaxy, all the way back into endless space —
or whether all that's a projection of my faith that I cannot be alone in
here, making all this up.
Is Nature substantial or just an apocalypse of the mind?
I can't get outside my senses, my concept, my humanness, to test
what they may be.
Idealism is frivolous.

To say Nature exists or not is one and the same.

God is no joke.

God doesn't, can't, compromise.

Nature is ironclad either way.

Without scientifically discovered laws (the human mind's penchant for reasonable investigation being an essential feature of its wonder and awe) firm in our minds, life is unlivable. To fall upwards, to stand on one's head, to be old before young and so on would only make a bad situation worse, compounding our confusion, which is as it is at least bounded by reliable parameters.

Our faith in Nature is perfect.

Each day we expect the sun to appear in the east and set in the west and ourselves to rise from bed in the morning and return to it at night. And we are not disappointed. Therefore there is breakfast, lunch, dinner, coherent conversation, joy and expectation, despair, panic, and practical activity. Our wheels and cogs are set to Nature's predictable plan. We are not ships tossed in stormy unpredictable waves. We're houses built on solid ground (but for the occasional flood, typhoon, hurricane, wildfire, earthquake). Thus we resist with denial and indignation any hint that Nature is unreliable. It must not be. And yet, despite the outright doubting or the willful or unwitting — and necessary — forgetting, all carpenters, wheelwrights, oil workers, bus drivers, construction workers, executives, and Wall Street financiers know the truth: Nature is no longer natural. We have become her partners. Yet natural laws remain in effect — which is perhaps the problem. Our ability to influence them, or even understand them closely enough, is small. And so Nature has her way with us. And, powerful as we think ourselves nevertheless to be, we stand before her drooping with confusion even as we bluster with confidence in our ability to provide solutions or wring our hands in woe at what we have wrought.

But in all this the question of whether Nature actually exists outside our minds remains open.

Our long human conversation has told us that Nature is a benign and permanent process, God the reality behind that process. Such a view seemed reasonable. We have had assurances. Previously outside the repeating picture in an eternity precariously elsewhere, God now speaks confusedly from within Job's whirlwind spinning in midst of perception. Nature is no more benign and permanent.

Reality is subject to doubt and revision. God's voice addresses us in strident tones in a vocabulary of unprecedented events and nightmarish futures, either passing judgment or inviting wonder, as we will. Thus the identity of God, Nature, and human is spoken more clearly than before, when the senses showed us a powerful and baffling world of shape, color, and fearful objects, opaque and uncontrollable, until reason, thought, and science contextualizing the senses into a large nonprofit summer camp, so that we understood the invisible, dispelled the superstitious, and gained control enough so that prayers from trembling pious lips became unnecessary and quaint. With reason and science grace brushed our eyelids. Taming nature we saw her loveliness without terror. Outlines disappeared — we saw patterns. We had no need to call on God though we sensed God more than before, within our own power to know and appreciate the wondrous complexity and ever-connected patterned detail.

Science is reverential and humble.

But engineering dominates.

The effects of culture: One.

Idealist philosophy takes its bent from Nature. Nature and spirit conspire to emancipate us. Mechanical changes inspire dualism. Such as small changes in our point of view. We see the shore from a moving boat, the clouds from an airplane window, the mountain through the thin and moving mists. Everything becomes a moving picture that brings with it the pleasures of illusion. Driving on the city streets we observe the show — men, women — talking, walking, styrofoam cups in hand, staring at personal screens — the hawker, the beggar, the traffic cop, the dogs on leashes, the fashion (no two outfits alike) — all detached from connection to us and so seen like apparitions, images, entertainments. We snap a photo. Our devices contains tens of thousands of such cloud-stored photos. Images commemorating events themselves become events when shared and viewed, chimerical substitutes for a living reality becoming increasingly fleeting abstract and forgettable. Thus the old false assumption that we exist becomes ever thinner and we increasingly doubt that the images we sift depict an actual former present we really lived. Yet we desperately love these photos of ourselves and our families. Looking at them brings smiles to our lips, tears to our eyes. In full color that can be easily enhanced and edited. We can

turn the photos upside down. We can crop them any way we wish.
We can make them into scrapbooks, greeting cards, calendars,
coffee mugs. Each photo is dated. It's location is noted. We travel.
The photos show our gradually changing faces against notable
scenery. The world flows by. But we (so we think) are here. Thus by
mechanical means we become observers of a spectacle:
Nature as backdrop.
We are not Nature.

Two.

Poets do far better with far less, evoking preternatural experience
from syllables' twitch, tiny pulsations within the soul. Here we find
actual air, sun, mountains, countryside, city, politics, passion, the
hero, the maiden—snatched from the world, lifted from the page,
swirling in the ear. Poets unhook things from their fixedness, pivot
in thought, spewing newness. They are heroically (if quietly, to
look at them no one would know) spun by history and the timeless,
addressing world with feeling, feeling with world, for without words
worlds and feelings press too forcefully, and pierce. An ordinary
person conforms thought to the things he proposes exist beyond
it. Poets conform things (they know they do not exist otherwise) to
thought. The one assumes the world is firm and given, the other
knows there is no world outside the fluid flexible fungible and
prophetic cast of thought and word.
The refractory world is ductile. Dust and stones are human.
Imagination makes the world usefully embraceable, placing it within
the scope of feeling, reflection, and love. Shakespeare dissolves
world in expression's solution. His imperial muse tosses fluid world
about like a bauble floated from hand to hand. He props the whole of
it behind any word that strikes his fancy at the moment, improvising
wildly within his paper-thin plots. He visits out-of-the-way places,
knits together the split-apart, shows subtle spiritual connections
plain. The magnitude of material things is relative. All objects shrink
and expand when words churned in spirit rule. Thus in his sonnets
birdsong and flowers are the beloved's shadow; time, which keeps
her from him, is his chest; suspicion an ornament; joy a box of
Kleenex, a well paved road, the curiosity that killed the cat, a jacket
worn by a night watchman, and all the cumbersome packaging in
which his order arrives so much pulchritude of invention.
Somewhere in all this a crow is eating a power bar.

His passion isn't just something he feels — it's a city, a terrorist attack, a newly opened outlet mall. It's no accident, nor does it suffer objectionable pomp nor furrow its brow in discontent, it doesn't worry about policy (that heretic that works on short-term contract) — it stands politically alone. His constancy is so great it makes the Pyramids seem a recent construction. His youth and his love are more dazzling than dawn. Her lips are foresworn, her eyes the break of day, which, when flashing in the evening, mislead morning.

Thus the passions of the poet derange Nature and violate the common sense for no apparent reason or useful purpose. The great are dwarfed. The small are magnified. He shakes the mountain, uprooting the pines and cedars upon it. He then plays soothing music, which cools down his brain that had been boiling in his skull. The spell then dissipates, and as the morning steals upon the night, melting the darkness, so do the senses begin to chase away the fumes that mantle reason and understanding, which begin to swell, and the approaching tide fills the shore that had been muddy and foul with clear and bracing waters. In such ways the poet plays the world like a lute, and asserts the predominance of the soul, despite all the bad news.

Three.

Thus the poet animates Nature with thought. She differs from the philosopher who proposes truth as her main end — while the poet's beauty is a shredding of truth into interior design. Ever-colorful and constantly shifting strings of luminosity bright in the listless afternoons as if suspended over waterways. Yet the philosopher no less than the poet subsumes whatever order and apparent relation between things into the austere dark corridors of thought.

"The problem of philosophy," according to Plato "is to find the unconditioned and absolute ground of the conditioned," a doomed search only a confused and misguidedly hopeful person without family or useful trade would conceive of. A great luxury for the alternatively-abled.

Philosophy proceeds on the faith that things make the sort of sense mind can apprehend. This would enable such minds to predict what happens next, thus reducing the natural terror such minds feel when things seem out of control.

We call the product of such efforts ideas.

Ideas are infinitely beautiful.

Thus both poets and philosophers are beautiful in their relation to truth, which is so elusive. Plato's and Aristotle's definitions are as imaginative as Sophocles' Antigone's passion. In both cases a spiritual life has been imposed by the mind onto Nature, matter has been dissolved by thought, and the pathetically vulnerable and temporary human being has penetrated Nature's vast mass with the informing soul, recognizing the soul itself as implicated therein, in harmony with all.

In physics a single formula explains a million disparate phenomena rendering the need for observation of particular phenomena moot and events corpse-like insignificances.

Four.

Science leads to doubt that matter exists at all.

Tutor said, "He who has never doubted the existence of matter has no aptitude for thought." For ideas are immaterial and never die. In their presence the material world seems foolishly inept and all but beside the point. A dream and a phantasy. We wait on the Olympus of the gods, far above the messiness below. We know we share in the experience of the supreme. "There are those there from everlasting, from the beginning, from before the beginning, before the earth. When He made the heavens they were already there, when He made the clouds, the fountains of the deep. They were there with Him even then and He asked them for advice."

Such are ideas.

Such heights can we humans reach through their grace.

Thus are we divine.

Ideas renew us, we become nimble and light, we walk on air, life is simple. There's no sickness no age no dying. Ideas never change. Justice and truth have legs. Nothing strains them. And we can know them! So we actually exist! We are immortal! We are important!Time and space slip away. What do they matter?

Five.

But religion and ethics — which are the imposition of ideas onto living, as though living could be made to conform to a pre-fab program — propose terrible effects on Nature, as if subsuming her under their baleful spell; missing her point thus falling apart without realizing you are falling apart, coming to a condition of dazed insanity, and celebrating the fact as higher truth. Ethics and religion differ: ethics is human duty in relation to all that is the case; religion

is human duty in relation to God, that is, to all that is not the case.
Religion includes the personality of God, language's self
contradiction.

Ethics insists that language makes sense. But both of these
perspectives step on Nature's toes. Religion says, "Look at all
this! It's merely a passing show. Look beyond it to what's eternally
here, that you can't see, but believe it, believe it." So disrespectful
to the seen and heard! Religion talks to ordinary people, saying
this, unlike philosophy and the higher thought, which speaks to the
educated classes, who have wasted their time on obscure books,
agreeing with one another about the condition of the world, but know
no better, only think more highly of themselves. So in churches
preachers say, "The world's corrupt! Vanity, vanity etc. Only God
is real! Only God knows for sure so you can know for sure. So
be sure to vote Republican (or any right wing party) because
these guys have your back, they know and love you. They too
believe." The religious have no use for Nature. Some of them even
hate her for her refusal to perform the end of time on command,
causing awkward talkbacks, elaborate embarrassed excuses, and
recalculation. They hate Nature because they know they are Nature
and recognize her volatility and basic unreliability in themselves,
which they abjure. They are rightfully terrified of their bodies, such
smells, such disgusting productions, such unattractiveness in aging,
such ignobility in decay.

They say of matter, as Michael Angelo said of beauty,
"It is the frail and weary weed in which Good addresses the soul
which he has called into time," and in this way they comfort and
congratulate themselves for the sin of having been born to sin. It
seems that motion, poetry, science, philosophy, and religion cause
us to believe that the dubious world is real. Culture is thus inherently
idealistic, putting humans at the center of things, like a pandemic
you can't avoid, though so much else is occurring. I love Nature as
children do. They don't name nor think of it. They have no context.

They merely expand into the warmth of the day, like melons or
corn. But they grow up and of necessity must place themselves in
a picture; because their minds are shaped by accumulated feelings
words and perceptions that seem to coalesce around an abiding
central emotional metaphor that produces in them a need to find
their sensible place. They think it over and conclude that what they

took to be real is not. They grow away from their soil-bound sun-drenched selves to selves built on their ideas. Children believe in the external world. It persuades them as myth. It speaks. Culture tells them this belief is trivial, there must be more. Aliveness can't be sufficient. There must be an add-on. So Nature must be suspect, and confidence in her, without teleology, must be misplaced.

The body ceases to be a trusted friend.

But this is at it should be, as reason requires. For philosophy and ethics depend on reason, as does progress and practical well-being. After all, the world occurs. Exists. It will nor stop nor slow for meaning. Virtue requires it be subordinated to the mind. Idealism sees the world in God.

The whole buzzing mess of it, with all its people, actions, destructions, creations, unresolved issues, screaming uncertainties, unrequited energies, atom after atom, act after act, can't just be chaos, painfully accumulated, oozing all over the scene, it must have order, beauty, sense, pattern, a picture painted by God on the canvas of eternity, for the contemplation of the peaceful soul.

Therefore the soul must stand aloof from the spectacle. True, religion's history, a human disaster, is itself a buzzing mess, but not to worry. Doctrines, contested miracles, crusades, inquisitions, tortured theology, no matter. The world's intolerable without some version of meaning, however unexamined its implications may be. With such meaning I can be disturbed or violent, satisfied or chagrined, with unbridled passion and full permission, for I stand somewhere, on the ground of an idea I do not recognize, accept, or reject, but feel underfoot, outside my body and the world in which it lives, as ideological bastion of nutriment.

Two Poems

Jesse Glass

The Shower

You stand behind the door wrapped in the protean arms of the shower,
The false rain crushing your locks to your head and the single curl
Drooling ephemeral gemstones down the bridge of your nose
That lacquer your lips, your breast, your belly, to whirl in a vortex beneath your toes
Around the silver cusp of the drain. He soothes you--this lover of uncertain shape
Caresses you before I have a chance, has secretly been where I can only hope
To be once or twice a week, yet every evening you dance lewdly with him
Innocently saying he helps you sleep, then hide yourself when you come to me, each limb
In its flannel sheath swims in the humid dark. I hate him
And his cords of light shattering upon your hair,
He (with his cobra head twisted upon the air,
And his hundred pin-prick mouths vomiting transient cleanliness
From the wallpaper trees, where he, with a wry hiss
Was installed decades before we ventured upon this scene),
Slants down behind plaster and lath, his vast bulk unseen;
He coils through the ancient dark to join the hidden source
Within the cloaca of the world, the first ambiguous force:
The menstruum of the night which yet falls purely in the light,

The solvent of blood and of poison, drowner of men, balm of blight,
This gushing confluence of molecules, hidden in aquifer, cistern and well
Laves and suffuses the curves of your body, burdens the nap of the stainless towel.

The New Motor. (1854) (1, 2)

1.
We know these revelations are
                    True:
That Mrs. Samantha Mettler of Hartford, Connecticut
Was given the New Dispensation in a dream
In which God's Eye blinked leaden tears
                    Upon
                        Her
                        Breasts
                            & a great voice boomed out in warning
                                Like a cannon across the countryside
                                Which was joined by the ineffable sound
                            Of Heavenly machines praising God
                                In the highest
                                & a carding machine rose
                                With the face of an angel
                                & bent its singing head
                                    Above her bed

How fondly, how constantly, how widely is this one beloved!
How beautiful is the influence this woman exerts!
Wherever she is she attracts! Her friends
Know no bounds to their affection for this one
& There is nothing which they would leave undone to gratify her!

That very night *The Society of Spirit Engineers* came
  Rapping through Reverend Spear's Mystic
Table: "The New Motor waits outside
Yr. Dimension. Hasten to build the body that will
Last 1000 years of copper plate & wire."

Brothers & Sisters

THE PHYSICAL SAVIOR OF THE RACE is now bolted
To a rock in Lynn, Massachusetts!

Mrs. Samantha Mettler, having traveled with her husband
At the direction of her holy dreams, felt
Her womb swell
& Odic forces clutch her womanly parts.
As she watched sunlight
Rake across the black box in the loins
Of our electric wonder

> She was thrown into the contractions
> Of childbirth
> & all the turbines in Lynn, Massachusetts
> Refused to turn, & mill men by the creek
> Heard *hallelujahs from the grindstones*
> *All that day!*

2.
So let the beautiful women kiss a cog
In the New Motor's cheek. Let them
Spread their legs & touch themselves
In the presence of the New Motor!

Come
Come
Come with me brother to the New Motor
On the hill.

Notice the copper tubing, the
Mouth rotors & generator shaft, the
Isinglass eyes & vibrations that run
Through the hinged hands when we drop to our knees together
> in prayer.

They who say they love you
Would clap blinders across your eyes

& lace you into a madman's restraining bed.
Newton was a madman. The spirits say:
"Man is a race horse running in the wrong direction,
The iron bit flipped upon his tongue."
Reverend Spear says: *Turn!*
        (Listen to me--
Mrs. Samantha Mettler birthed
Free energy for every American who believes!)

3.
Believe with us, then
            Brothers, Sisters
Come & pray, for
It hears all,
Knows what you know,
Will dance like brilliant Christ
Across a red plain. . .will
Never lie down. . .won't wear out. . .no
Sweatshop awaits it. . .no vultures
Dig in its side. . .no
Sheriff can lock it up. . .
No war destroy it.

I feel strong already
            Brothers, Sisters
Long live FREE ENTERPRISE!
& Entropy is bound
To plunder the crypts
Of Europe
Like a comet-headed Jackal,
While America
Will rise on the backs
Of Seraphim & Cherubim:
A domed & crystal
City in the morning
        Air!

We must confidently assert that the advent of the science
Of all sciences, the philosophy of all philosophies, &

The art of all arts has now fairly commenced. The child
Is born; not long hence he will go alone. Then he will
Dispute with the doctors in the Temples of Science!

4.

Weep not!
Weep not!

For

The New Motor has risen from us
Brothers,
Sisters,

And in a mighty crucifixion
The coils and copper boxes of its physical body,
The isinglass eyes
& hinged fingers and
Toes
Were transfigured at the hands of the
Unbelievers of Randolph, (3)
Into mortal dross;
And all because Elias Brown was allowed
Among us,
He who promised
To join us in prayer & service
Found pleasure in Mrs. Mettler, our Holy
Conductress, yet denounced us in the streets of that Sodom
Of New York state, and in its newspaper
Profaned all the mysteries of which he partook.
I was not there at the final hour
When Reverend Spear was turned out
From his sanctuary in night clothes,
And rock-throwing children chased Mrs. Mettler
Into the arms of a protecting Sheriff.
Yet I heard
Of the final glory
Of THE MECHANICAL SAVIOR
OF THE RACE--
How it faced its Persecutors

With mystic calm, extended its copper arms
To embrace them & the starry sky,
But felt instead the sledgehammer and the ax. Our martyred child
Prepares a way for us in Heaven.
                                    &
Though the *Society of Spirit Engineers*
Spells out that another can't be built,
                                Do not weep, brother!
                                Do not weep, sister!
It clatters its welcome like a telegraph in the abyss,
And heats the cold void between the stars
With its electric breath! Thank God
The principles which have been presented
& the philosophy which has been communicated
are beyond the reach of the mob & cannot be harmed
By the slanders of the pulpit or the misrepresentations
Of the press. Truth crushed to earth shall rise again:
The eternal years of God are ours!

Notes

1. Initially based on an entry in Leslie A, Shepard's *The
   Encyclopedia of Occultism & Parapsychology Vol. 1.* (1985), which gives
   a concise retelling of the events at High Rock, Lynn Massachusetts,
   the scandal of the 'birth' of the New Motor and its signs of 'life', and its
   consequent destruction by a mob at Randolph, New York in 1855.

2. Excerpted from The Raftsman's Journal. (Clearfield, Pa.),
   Aug. 30, 1854.

...Rev. John M. Spear's "New Era"....The New Era, a spiritual paper,
publishes an article about what is called the "Electrical Motor," or "New
Savior". "The New Era speaks of its deep satisfaction that the world is, by
and by, to be blessed beyond conception by this physical Savior, through
whose instrumentality a permanent material basis shall be laid for true
spiritual salvation."

The new "Savior" is a machine which has been constructed at Lynn, Mass., by the Spiritualists, which they claim to be semi-mechanical and semi-human. It has been denominated a "New Motive Power" and cost $2,000 to construct it. The New Era remarks that the Electric Motor is an exact correspondence of the human body, at least as far as involuntary motion is concerned. It was constructed under Spear's direction, and chiefly at Spear's expense. In the New Era of July 5th, we find a vision had by J. Wolcott, which develops what is expected to be accomplished by this machine. It appeared to grow in size, and "threw off from itself small machines after its own pattern" and these " in turn threw off a multitude of other little ones." Then he says—

"Next there appeared a movement among the machines, and the larger ones, which were now fully developed, moved away over the plain into the distance. In their path stood a great number of churches, of every size and variety, from the diminutive Methodist Chapel up to the stately Gothic Minster and St. Paul's Cathedral. But the machines did not turn out of their course at all, running over and through those temples, [and] completely demolished them to heaps of worthless rubbish."

3. On the destruction of the New Motor at Randolph, New York, and Spear's sole description of the 'mob' see Neil B. Layman's Doctoral dissertation The Life Of John Murray Spear: Spiritualism and Reform in Antebellum America. (Ohio State University Graduate School, 1973. Pgs. 200-201.)

4.

"...But the renewal of the work at Randolph had barely begun when Spear and his associates discovered that there was considerable popular resistance to spiritualist encroachment in Randolph, and that western New Yorkers were not so tolerant as the more urbane citizens of Lynn, Massachusetts. A mob of residents '...under the cover of night,' as Spear reported, entered the temporary building where the machine was housed, and 'tore out the heart of the mechanism. Trampled [it] beneath their feet, and scattered it to the four winds....'"

Layman offers a further amplification of Wolcott's vision as reported in the July 5th, 1854 of the New Era (see above) of the consequences of the proliferation of these machines. Stripped of the religious language, notice how similar it is to reactions by modern opponents of nano-technology with their predictions of 'gray sludge':

"In one instance a reader sent a note saying that he had had a vision in which he saw masses of people laughing at the machine. But the machine then spawned thousands of identical machines which commenced to go about breaking up great cathedrals while the people wept. The figure of Christ then appeared upon the horizon and said to the people, 'Behold I bring you glad tidings of great joy, which shall be to all people. The long sought philosopher's stone is at length discovered and all the earth shall have a portion.'...."

The trap of visibility: a brief glance at the work of Douglas Woolf

Ian Brinton

In 1975 the French publisher Gallimard presented to the light of the world Michael Foucault's *Surveiller et punir: Naissance de la prison* translated into English two years later by Alan Sheridan under the title *Discipline and Punish: the Birth of the Prison*. Foucault's analysis of the surveillance of prisoners within a purpose-built civic construction looked closely at the prison system devised in 1843 by Jeremy Bentham and accorded the name Panopticon:

> We know the principle on which it was based: at the periphery, an annular building; at the centre, a tower; this tower is pierced with wide windows that open onto the inner side of the ring; the peripheric building is divided into cells, each of which extends the whole width of the building; they have two windows, one on the inside, corresponding to the windows of the tower; the other, on the outside, allows the light to cross the cell from one end to the other. All that is needed, then, is to place a supervisor in a central tower and to shut up in each cell a madman, a patient, a condemned man, a worker or a schoolboy. By the effect of backlighting, one can observe from the tower, standing out

precisely against the light, the small captive shadows in
the cells of the periphery. They are like so many cages, so
many small theatres, in which each actor is alone, perfectly
individualized and constantly visible.

As Foucault went on to point out this system reverses two of the
three principles that had been the groundwork of dungeons: to
enclose, to deprive of light and to hide. Whilst ensuring that the first
of these, that controlled by the lock and key, remains the other two
are eliminated:

Full lighting and the eye of a supervisor capture better than
darkness, which ultimately protected. Visibility is a trap.

The effectiveness of this method of controlling people was
of course central to George Orwell's post-war dystopian picture of
what life would be like in 1984. Rooms are dominated by televisions,
telescreens, which receive and transmit simultaneously. A large
metal plaque on the wall of each room commands a view and 'there
was of course no way of knowing whether you were being watched
at any given moment'. The result of this monitoring was that people
had to live, 'from habit that became instinct' under the assumption
that every sound you made and every shade of thought which
passed over your face was being scrutinised. In his 1962 novel *One
Flew Over the Cuckoo's Nest* Ken Kesey recognized the powerful
possibilities of this form of surveillance when he created his mental
home, his 'Institution of Psychology', his prison for those who don't
fit into society but who voluntarily desire to be inside this safe-house.
Here Big Nurse spends her day in the glass-fronted Nurses' Station
looking out at the patients and, in the words of the narrator Chief
Bromden, 'she wields a sure power that extends in all directions on
hairlike wires too small for anybody's eye but mine'. Bromden has
been there a few years now and he sees her 'sit in the centre of this
web of wires like a watchful robot'. Big Nurse knows every second
'which wire runs where and just what current to send up to get the
result she wants'. Three years before the publication of Kesey's
novel Douglas Woolf's 1959 novel *Fade Out* appeared from Grove
Press and one of its central characters, Dick Twombly, finished
working in a bank and went to spend his retirement years with his

daughter Kate where he had 'to learn the rules of the house'. These involved learning that 'Kate ran everything after a pattern, beginning with the order in which the family woke and continuing with the order in which they occupied the single bathroom'. The dystopian prison world of Kate's New York apartment is emphasised by its positioning as it faced 'away from the street, toward another apartment house close by' and there was 'nothing anyone could look at except TV'. When Kate goes on to get rid of her father by having him admitted into an old peoples' 'Home' (he has been embarrassing her by spending 'free time' in the local park chatting to kids) she attempts to keep him trapped in the house during the morning that she is making the final preparations for his incarceration; she hasn't informed him yet that it will take will place that afternoon! Her tone of voice is closely linked to the tone with which Big Nurse in Kesey's novel controls **her** patients: there is an insidious inflection which suggests that the imprisonment is for the good of the patient:

> "I think you better stay inside, don't you today? Why don't we turn on the set?"

Before Twombly's daughter sets off supposedly to the drugstore she waits at the door 'until she was sure Mr. Twombly was watching, at least facing the set, before she opened it'. Arriving at the Home later that day Twombly sees that it is 'a rectangular two-story building with no roof you could see, might have been anyone's home ten times enlarged'. It had a fluorescent five-digit number nailed over the door and as he follows his daughter and son-in-law 'up the wide cement ramp' Mr. Twombly notes that 'all the pink shades in the downstairs picture windows were drawn'. The upstairs shades were raised but no faces were to be seen looking out. When they arrive at one of the lounges all Twombly can see is the TV:

> Much larger than Kate's it was built into the wall, or rather into an imitation fireplace with a real mantel of knickknacks above and the bright picture where the fire would have been.

The ladies in the room are all sitting in low easychairs in rows four-deep and they react uniformly as 'they all turned their heads to the light in the hall'. The pervading atmosphere of that day-room, that comfortable lounge, foreshadows the institution that Claude Squires works in at the beginning of Woolf's 1962 novel *Wall to Wall*. Arriving for work at the 'nut-house' as one of the doctors who works there calls it, in the early morning Squires notes that at that hour of the day 'the password was lethargy' but also that part of the terror of the 'home' was 'that it did seem almost peaceful here, more peaceful than anywhere else, than anywhere'. In this sedated atmosphere nobody runs on the grounds and along the drives 'the bread, the meat, the milk, the laundry trucks glided noiselessly by like peddled things'. This tranquil imprisonment is closely woven into a distrust of language and an encouraged reliance upon clichéd statements. As Squires moves around the south wing and 'over the half-hearted croquet court' he enters the 'men's domain' and takes a seat at a table: 'He was working now'. One of the inmates, Mr. Harris, asks Squires if he has read the morning newspaper yet and holds it out to him. As a response to Squires saying that he hasn't, a sternly emphasised piece of advice is offered:

> "Don't read it," Mr. Harris said, folding the paper once more and sliding it under his rear. "It will only upset you, son."

When Squires suggests that it is 'a wicked paper', a phrase in which the tone of the adjective has a humorous awareness of being an over-the-top piece of banter, Harris interrupts him with his theory of language:

> "It's the big black words that do it. The little grey ones don't matter very much, they're just fill-ins they take everyday from the wires. They concentrate their poison in the big black words, where it will radiate. Of course if you read the little stories too you've got sure proof that every word they wrote above, themselves, was a fat black lie, but by then you've absorbed a thousand greyer ones, and where and how to check on those? This way the mind deteriorates. The best way you can save yourself is not to read it, son."

The dangers which lurk in any seeking for information, any questioning of the status quo, any enquiry that might entail a focus upon an understanding of the individual's awareness of his own place in the world , are constantly emphasised by the prison system. In the well-run world of *One Flew over the Cuckoo's Nest* one of the patients, Mr. Taber, unwisely asks a question about the medication he is being persuaded/compelled to take every day, those little red capsules that accompany his vitamins. The attractive young nurse who is subordinate to Big Nurse answers with a tone of veiled threat:

> "It's just medication, Mr. Taber, good for you. Down it goes, now."
> "But I mean what kind of medication. Christ, I can see that they're pills-"
> "Just swallow it all, shall we, Mr. Taber – just for me?" She takes a quick look at the Big Nurse to see how the little flirting technique she is using is accepted, then looks back at the Acute. He still isn't ready to swallow something he don't know what is, not even just for her.
> "Miss. I don't like to create trouble. But I don't like to swallow something without knowing what it is, neither. How do I know this isn't one of those funny pills that makes me something I'm not?"
> "Don't get upset, Mr. Taber – "
> "Upset? All I want to know, for the lova Jesus – "
> But the Big Nurse has come up quietly, locked her hand on his arm, paralyses him all the way down to the shoulder. "That's all right, Miss Flynn," she says. "If Mr Taber chooses to act like a child, he may have to be treated as such. We've tried to be kind and considerate with him. Obviously, that's not the answer. Hostility, hostility, that's the thanks we get. You can go, Mr Taber, if you don't wish to take your medication orally."

The menace lurking beneath the surface of the passage is grotesque as flirtatious cliché moves towards covert threat. Whereas in Woolf's world Mr Harris slides the newspaper 'under his rear', a comic inference of Joycean proportions, Kesey's threat of alternative methods of being medicated are more harshly obvious and the threat is devoid of humour.

The only way to avoid the penetrating glance of the system would appear to be to act secretly and when Mr Twombly uses an ashtray for a secret cigarette which he indulges in after his daughter has gone off to work he takes it into the bathroom to dump the contents into the toilet, flushing it:

> This was a subterfuge he had used as a boy at home, and it reminded him that he would have to open his window when he got back.

In similar fashion he takes off his left shoe and removes the arch support from it:

> He took out the wad of travellers cheques, rapidly counted them. They were all there, $1, 740 worth. Fitting the roll in his shoe again, he was reminded of the first money he had saved as a boy in Baltimore. It had been his runaway money, and he had cached it in a hole his doorknob had dug in the plaster of his wall. On the day his fund had reached an even dollar he had pushed it too far in, and it had fallen behind the wall. All that winter he had tried to get it out, using fish hooks, chewing gum, coat hangers, without success. He had never got over being troubled by the thought of that money probably still lying in there unused, never in fact had quite got over regretting that he had never run away.

The satiric image here is of the world of the banking system where money is put away for safe-keeping which encourages adherence to the accepted mode of living: accumulation of objects and 'putting things by for a rainy day'. The image of the hidden place that is static, the hidey-hole that doesn't travel with you, had occurred to Daniel Defoe back in 1722 when the hero of his novel *Colonel Jack* looks for 'some hole in a tree' in which he can hide his money 'till I should have occasion for it.' The young man climbs up a tree to reach a hole and 'placed my treasure there and was mighty well satisfied with it.' However, he clumsily drops his 'little parcel' and discovers that it has 'fallen in quite out of my reach':

> …so that, in a word, my money was quite gone, irrevocably lost – there could be no room so much as to hope ever to

> see it again, for it was a vast great tree.

Defoe's picture of banking has a wonderfully acute sense of the system as the young Jack discovers that the tree is hollow and 'had a great open place in the side of it close to the ground, as old hollow trees often have' and hence acts like an early ATM as Jack can retrieve his savings with 'inexpressible joy'.

In *Fade Out* Mr Twombly takes his savings with him in his shoe and treads his way to the ghost-town of Harding where he and his friend Ed (Behemoth) Brown will set up a new home for themselves, one in which they are responsible for their own lives. Dedicated to Robert Creeley the journey undergone by these two pensioners in *Fade Out* is exhilarating as they make their escape from New York and enforced conformity through streets, apartments and dangerous parks. They travel by Bloodhound bus down to Baltimore on their way to their intended destination of Phoenix, Arizona, Dick Twombley's choice of future home with its sound of resurrection. They hitch-hike a lift on a Navajo truck with Many Goats and his family and never reach Phoenix but instead discover Harding, a place that gives the impression of not being subject to the immediate pressures of time. As Paul Metcalf put it in *Broken Field Runner, A Douglas Woolf Notebook* (The Jargon Society, 1972)

> But still, for all the sideshow attractions, it is the matter
> of pace: zipping, stuttering, halting and whizzing, through
> the mainshow – to the prize at the end, a real sweeting: a
> glorious ghost town, abandoned home for abandoned men.

The prison break-out in *One Flew over the Cuckoo's Nest* is more immediately dramatic and the main protagonist is set up like a hero from a western. The psychopathic 'gunslinger', R.P. McMurphy, takes on the system of the Panopticon by breaking through the windows: he enters the ward of 'rabbits' and becomes the 'wolf'. Unlike the screen heroes such as Clint Eastwood's 1964 cowboy in 'A Fistful of Dollars' McMurphy will lose his bid for freedom but his determination not to remain as the passive object of observation will enable the narrator, Chief Bromden, to follow his example of non-cooperation. Bromden, the disinherited Indian, will escape:

> I ran across the grounds in the direction I remembered seeing the dog go, towards the highway. I remember I was taking huge strides as I ran, seeming to step and float a long ways before my next foot struck the earth, I felt like I was flying. Free. Nobody bothers coming after an AWOL....I been away a long time.

Douglas Woolf's *Notes for an Autobituary* was published in the second issue of Tom Raworth's magazine *Outburst* in 1963, and when nine years later Paul Metcalf titled his short account of Woolf's publications *Broken Field Runner* he took this from his own words on that short piece of writing. Metcalf referred to the author as the 'little scat back, the broken field runner (everything fluid, kinetic, variable, myriad decisions reached instantly), leaving the big guys flat-footed'. Metcalf went on to add that so many of the heroes in Woolf's novels are like that: 'quick, adept, good-natured guys, who step lively, skipping through the malign absurdities of their world, believing, somehow, in the purpose of it all, that somewhere there is a pattern that makes sense – and wind up plucking, if anything at all, a mean russet, with dark wartish blotches, by way of reward.' The tone of this writing anticipates the comments made by Ed Dorn in his introduction to the 1993 Black Sparrow collection of Woolf's writings, *Hypocritic Days and Other Tales* when he referred to America as

> ...a smug, hardhearted, unforgiving nation of jackals, which forever slaps itself on its back over how generous, selfless and idealistic it is. It is the most preposterous propaganda barrage since Goebbels ran an office, in bloodier and more interesting times.
> You go to the window. You look out at the immense night. You see the plough, the dipper, you see the fish and you see the net. Every thing blood and bone ever needed is shown and displayed in the sky. You can hunker down and pay the mortgage, and save yourself a lot of trouble, or you can see the show. There actually isn't any other choice. For a mere traveller has no access to the haunts.

In Woolf's novel *Ya!* started in 1965 and published in 1971, the protagonist, a penniless author called Al, leaves his

job and hitchhikes West across the Cascade Mountains to spend
Christmas with his daughter Joan who lives with her aunt and uncle
who certainly hunkered down. Al encounters a blizzard, a snow-
slide which blocks all traffic; he escapes from friendly western
drivers whose wheels can only spin; he takes to the woods on foot
accompanied by the decision that you've got to 'Keep on walking'.
And so he does, buoyed by the banks and drifts, resting on tree
limbs, skidding into hidden gravel banks, worrying about tripping
over buried snow ploughs or telephone wires. In the details of the
interstate journey we are led to recognise that if a public gaze is
a form of imprisonment then sleeping in a snow-bound hemlock
tree is both privacy and freedom. and when he does need to stop
for the night in his temporary, snow-bound, 'house' he thinks of
'those drivers huddled behind their wheels, chewing gum and LSD,
listening to their radios and heaters.'

When Douglas Woolf's wife, Sandra Bremen, wrote her
'After Words' to that Black Sparrow Press edition of *Hypocritic Days
and Other Tales* in 1993 she quoted from a late poem of his:

> One of these Days I may
> just run off into the
> Sun
> you can look for me there

She went on to say that her husband's 'totemic identification with
the wolf provided...an explanation of his life habits, including moving
constantly, as a loner, dedicated fiercely to a family that moved with
him'.

In the concluding pages of *Ya!* as Al and Joan escape from
the wagon in which Auntie Doris and Uncle Roy are taking them to
a cattle show in Dallas, the father gives his daughter some clear
advice about making the jump:

> "We'll wait for the next curve...When you hit the ground, roll
> away like a ball."

They land ok and keep on walking before reaching a small canyon:

> There were no hemlocks back here, so he chose a young

pine. He showed her how to recline on a bough, using higher boughs for arm support. The niches were not as convenient down near the bottom, but he found her a good one. He found himself another nearby, with one arm branch. Hemlocks were better, of course. Leaning back, closing his eyes, he relaxed tentatively. The temperature felt just right in here.

When the British poet and critic J.H. Prynne wrote about Douglas Woolf's fiction as being 'the absolute prose of our time, so full of wit and grace and so clear of stupor and depravity that the elation it produces is simply without parallel' one is tempted to turn to the last lines of *Ya!* Joan turns to her father and says with a sigh, "This is wild" and her father replies "Yes, it is".

Conjure by Rae Armantrout
(Wesleyan University Press)

Ian Brinton

A world of integrity in which a whole life can be felt as a continuation in which one part proceeds understandably from another prompts Rae Armantrout not to be 'first on one side, / then the other'. To conjure is to permit a magical process in which the inevitability of synthesis comes as a joy of surprise and Heraclitean movement though the stream permits 'mouth and tail' to have 'one thought'.

For a poet whose attention to 'verbal constructs' permits the re-writing, the re-cadencing of language, words can be salvaged and replaced 'unlike my flesh' which in the inexorable movement of time shifts and changes in one direction only. For the poet 'care' is 'long-term' rather than 'acute' as the words that form the moment of stillness on a page can be looked at again by the poet herself as by the reader over the years:

> Words can be compared
>
> with moments,
> houses, trees, wires
> wires, trees, houses.

The very placing of the word within the construct is but a moment
on the starting-grid as they stand 'on their marks'. They may for
that one moment remain 'Still', as foot-prints on a page, before the
poet looks and thinks again to recognise the inevitable sense of
'overlap'. That second syllable is itself a conjuration, an awareness
of one movement of water overriding another, as Charles Tomlinson
was aware in his 1967 poem 'Swimming Chenango Lake'. Perhaps
it is no accident that Tomlinson was the first British poet to alert the
reading public in England to what had been happening for a few
years in America when he contributed his short Black Mountain
Poets anthology to the early 1964 issue of Ian Hamilton's *the
Review*:

> There is a geometry of water, for this
> 　　　Squares off the clouds' redundancies
> And sets them floating in a nether atmosphere
> 　　　All angles and elongations: every tree
> Appears a cypress as it stretches there
> 　　　And every bush that shows the season,
> A shaft of fire. It is a geometry and not
> 　　　A fantasia of distorting forms, but each
> Liquid variation answerable to the theme
> 　　　It moves away from, plays before:
> It is a consistency, the grain of the pulsating flow.

As a poet Rae Armantrout moves her eyes 'to make time' and sees
the world around her with the newness of taking a measure and
creating a duplicate: for *her* poetic clarity is a disruptive experience.
The ironies within this perception of the world are both rich and
rewarding as well as being deeply unsettling as in 'Pose'.

> So the problem we pose
> is how to create an intelligent
> 　　　　　　　agent
> and then prevent it
> from destroying this world?

Borrowed from medieval French, *poser*, and Late Latin pausāre
(to halt or rest) the verb/noun of the poem's title becomes a form

of questioning: the stillness of a 'pose' becomes the unsettling active interrogation of a question 'posed'. The linguistic intricacy, playfulness even, of these definitions forms a prologue to how terrifying a dystopian over-view of human activity can be:

> "Content monitoring
> that required the AI's
> intentional states
> to be transparent
> might not be feasible
> for all architectures."

As the initial words 'create' and 'intelligent' merge into the language of positive care, 'monitoring' and 'transparent', we witness the horrors of a warfare that will use an expectation of health with the certainty of death: a surgical strike!

Behind the sensuous particularity of Rae Armantrout's poems which depend upon the specific social relations in which they occur there is a delicate balance of wry humour and resilience that reminds one of those Blackhawk Island poems of Lorine Niedecker. Again it was Charles Tomlinson who, in his contribution to the 1983 collection of tributes, *The Full Note* (Interim Press), had referred to Niedecker's poems as being 'not the fruit of an anxious isolation' but 'rather points of patience' and of course in 'Section 12' of Louis Zukofsky's 'A' she had been characterized by the poet as 'a rich sitter'. There are echoes of Niedecker's quiet understanding of stillness and movement in Armantrout's 'Drift':

> An armoured dragonfly drifts
> from tree to tree and back
> all afternoon
>
> the way I walk into a room
> and pause,
> not knowing what I came for

The adjective describing the insect locates it in a measured sense of 'thereness' whilst the verb that immediately follows it ends the line with both movement and openness. This drift possesses a rhythmic balance between space and time: a landscape of 'tree to tree' becomes placed within 'all afternoon'. In Niedecker's own 1967 poem, 'Wintergreen Ridge' our movement is guided by signs:

> Where the arrows
> of the road signs
> lead us:

> Life is natural
> in the evolution
> of matter

The reader's journey becomes a confluence of history, physical sensation, memory and landscape and it will lead to the discovery that 'wintergreen' is 'grass of parnassus' allowing the poet to move from particular observation of the natural world to a sense of 'order' which she perceives within it.

To conjure is to make a compact (*con* + *jurare*) as in swearing together and the poet recognises the relation between a quest for newness and a truthful awareness of what has gone before. Rae Armantrout's poem 'Structures' begins in 'a moment' as 'each poem is a new door / opening in a wall' before recognising that we carry ourselves with us as the hallway it leads to

> seems familiar
> as does the eeriness of recognition.

> I look up to see leaves, thronged at the window,
> lambent,
> and think maybe there

Lullabies in the Real World by Meredith Quartermain

Peter Hughes

Lullabies in the Real World is a book of poems cast as a train journey across Canada, from west to east. The lullabies, however, are far from soothing. In spite of the compelling rhythmic movement of the lines we are constantly confronted with tough slabs and nuggets of 'Real World' which are presented to remind us that Canada (and by extension the world) is largely made out of greed, and at the expense of others. Many voices are invoked in the course of this journey. These include those of Homer, Blake, T.S.Eliot, William Carlos Williams, Robin Blaser and bpNichol. Meredith Quatermain also provides a good deal of detail regarding the history of the north American continent. She is particularly keen to dispel the myth of the heroic colonizer:

> ...heroes felling forest
> all winter long
>
> the champion railways
> the brave department stores
> the churches
> the sawmills

the shingle mills
the flour mills

as though Mi'kmaq
had not governed here
civilized
cultivated
for 10,000 years

(from 'Smoke stack billowing', p.79)

I like the way that the grammatical ambivalence of the two words and line 'civilized / cultivated' slows down our reading and makes renewed demands on our attention.
10,000 years is a long time but these poems take us a lot further back than that. Some of the oldest rock on Earth (not counting bits of meteorite which go back 7 billion years and were formed in other solar systems) is to be found in Canada. It's about 4 billion years old. Quatermain gestures towards this staggering antiquity in lines such as:

Bare heaving sea bottoms
weathered layers

(from 'Letter to bp Crossing the Rockies', p. 21)

or the even more memorable:

spruce shagged
granite shield back
of giant turtle jagged lichened

(from 'Lost human', p. 33)

These references to old geologies, geomorphologies and myths are not there for decoration, of course. They inspire a kind of awe and, more significantly, throw into relief the petty awe-free depredations of human beings upon the land since precontact times.

Lullabies in the Real World begins with a section called 'Rockabye' and we're on the train rattling its way out of Vancouver as evening falls:

> ...trainwave train shadow
> shunt clunk shadeland shadfly shamble-shanks
> rubbishy gulch-track gleam to river sidle
> warehouse after depot after shed after chute
> after silo after crane after...

(from 'Unreal to real', p.13)

You can see and hear and feel the messy world going past, speeding up, too fast to process. This first poem concludes with a more visionary moment, connecting us to more ancient celebrations and spiritual investigations. Our sense of who we are comes adrift, slips away. And look at the wonderful work being done by the last word quoted below, one-footed, precarious, as the train goes over points perhaps in a new direction:

> Rockabye, lost tonight
> rockabye, wheely
> clackity skulls rattle our masks
> when the train hops.

(from 'Unreal to real', p.13)

The poem has made the hop of the train resonate with a moment of ritual dance and this is not the only moment in the book that had me remembering Hart Crane and his north American epic, *The Bridge*. So we have cultural continuity throughout the text alongside the shifting physical continuities of the land itself.

One thing this book does is thresh out such continuities in the context of environmental and political degradation in this catastrophic phase of late Capitalism. Everything must be called into question and tested. Is it conducive to future well-being or not? The title of the second poem, 'On a pushing shifting thought-train', is suggestive of such dynamics. So is its third line: 'follow, don't follow, make it new'. Where are we? Well, we're moving so fast it's hard to tell! But the constant rhythmic onward thrust of the lines communicates a sense of urgency: we are hurtling headlong towards extinction and there is no longer any time to lose.

> Where are you going
> Oh human through burnt trees?

> (from 'Letter to Self', p.17)

Now and again through the text we catch glimpses of a more primal vision, perhaps a mode of being and perceiving more in tune with the natural cycles of the planet:

> I would a stargazer
> would a bison-memory be

> (from 'To the Un World', p. 18)

But such moments are not allowed to hover peacefully as disengaged poeticisms. They are surrounded by fraught reminders of our precarious state, by the dangers of human extinction. The latter is neatly evoked in the unimaginable 'Beethovenlessness' at the very end of 'Pyramid Falls' (p.19).

Lullabies in the Real World is an urgent and bracing book. It is frank and artful, riddled with both hope and despair. Meredith Quartermain is to be congratulated for bringing such timely riches to our shuddering tables.

Performing the Real: Miriam Nichols' biography of Robin Blaser

Meredith Quartermain

Among west coast poets in both Canada and the United States, Robin Blaser stands as a beacon, a singular landmark. His poetic journey and influence began in San Francisco in the 1950s with close associates Robert Duncan and Jack Spicer – their triumvirate of poetic vision and voice became known as the San Francisco Renaissance, influencing a wide community in the Bay area. When they were included in Don Allen's epoch-defining anthology *The New American Poetry 1945-1960*, their influence spread across the U.S.

In 1966, Blaser became a dual citizen when he moved to Canada and took a professorship at British Columbia's Simon Fraser University. This enabled him to establish his own turf apart from Duncan's and Spicer's spheres of influence, and to articulate not only his own distinguished poetic voice, but also a deeply nuanced vision of the role a poet and poetry play in the world at large. As such, his collected essays, *The Fire* (2006), and *The Astonishment Tapes: Talks on Poetry and Autobiography* (2015) (originally recorded in 1974), make essential reading for both poets and philosophers.

Throughout Blaser's career, he remained an important

figure both south and north of the border; as Nichols has remarked, his close literary connections include Charles Bernstein, George Bowering, Robert Creeley, Rachel Blau DuPlessis, Kevin Killian, Daphne Marlatt, Steve McCaffery, Erin Mouré, bpNichol, Michael Ondaatje, Sharon Thesen, Phyllis Webb, and many others.

Blaser's vision of the public world and one's individual agency within it remains an outstanding contribution to philosophical, political and artistic discourses and their interrelationships. Nichols' biography skillfully introduces the reader to all its key elements, making the book an excellent starting point for anyone interested in Blaser's poetry and thought. Today, in an era of retrenchment to fascisms, Blaser's thinking and methodology remain highly relevant, and offer ways for heterogeneous cultures to share common spaces respectfully instead of destructively. Even in his earliest essays, such as "The Fire" (1967) Blaser saw that what we view as the public world, public reality, had been severely diminished and cheapened, reduced merely to commercial exchanges. As Nichols puts it, Blaser wanted a correction to "the chronic ubiquity of the desire to be seen and heard – twisted . . . in celebrity culture and in violent grabs for power and respect from the streets to heads of state" (149). He wanted an alternative to "this constant din of thwarted egos" and instead called for the poet to enter

> an ongoing conversation that is the human way of gathering the world up. Entry to that conversation requires intense listening (this, rather than wealth, is the price of the ticket in the land of poetry): the poet addresses a shareable world of common concerns, not one of private fantasy or personal or collective will, and this requires much attentive scholarship. (149)

Most importantly the world that we bring into being through such practices is a much richer, much wiser place to be.

In his habit of interspersing his lines and ideas among the voices of many other thinkers, Blaser's poetry as well as his prose reflect this practice of intense listening and the attitude of being in conversation. In a later essay, "The Recovery of the Public World" (which became the hallmark of his work and the subject of a 1995 literary conference in Vancouver), Blaser noted how the reductivism of various modern disciplines such as sociology and economics leave the imagined public world empty of meaning, our lives similarly diminished. "Ah, the recovery of the public world, then. How can we uncover its disappearance in the tawdry?" he asked (Blaser, *The Fire* 85). We must educate ourselves in the great events of the history of human consciousness, he argued, including all the traditions of myths, the arts, and religions, which currently have been forgotten in favour of "scientism" and technological wizardry. We must find our way to a public space based on excellence, one in which we recognize and imagine ourselves in a condition of contrariety: in a "relationship to the otherness of persons, things, and the world. This process of relationship in contrariety and otherness is the fundamental activity of artistic discourse" (*The Fire* 80-81).

Blaser began his life far from the privilege and means that normally give access to such traditions. Born in 1925 in Denver, Colorado, Blaser spent much of his childhood in rural and small-town Idaho in a family who were mainly railroad workers. His literary biography, then, is doubly interesting in that it examines how such an erudite writer carefully recreated himself from his humble beginnings. "Blaser constructed identity by making his households into strong exoskeletons," Nichols tells us; "in an undated notebook he writes: 'the constant awareness of clothing, furniture—The need for these as they reflect some indefinable quality. Always, the quality outside the person, a building of the man in externals" (58). He was constantly sewing, painting, and decorating.

Blaser himself believed, as Nichols notes, that "the story of a life is also the story of a world and that such stories are the stuff of poetry. Nothing mattered more to him than poetry, and his life story is inextricable from its working out of a poetic practice" (7). Thus, Nichols weaves "three narrative lines" through the course of the book: "Blaser's personal story, his social context, and his ventures in poetry" (7).

Nichols herself, a professor of English for many years, is highly qualified to write this first well-thought-out biography. A former student and life-long personal friend of Blaser's, she has also edited his collected poems, *The Holy Forest*; his collected essays, *The Fire*; and the transcription of his 1974 talks on autobiography, *The Astonishment Tapes*. In addition, she has written and lectured widely on the poets and poetics of the late 20th century, notably in her collection *Radical Affections: Essays on the Poetics of the Outside* (2010).

Nichols is an accomplished scholar, and the biography is based on her extensive study of both published sources and unpublished archival materials such as letters and notebooks, all of which are listed for ease of reference. These materials inform her narrative; they never overwhelm or clutter it. Moreover, Nichols has skillfully divided the text with headings into short well-focused sections that enable readers with different interests to zero in on the sections that interest them and skip the ones that don't. Overall, her prose is highly readable, and her language lively and fresh. Most importantly, the biography continually makes connections between Blaser's life and specific poems or parts of them, and situates Blaser's poetics in the arguments and conversations of their decades.

One of the most important chapters for me is the one entitled "Big Poetry and the Recovery of the Public World." Nichols defines "big poetry" as "Dantean poetry," meaning poetry which envisions a world of differently situated actors and knowledges in conversation with one another, in which the poet has a middling, not a defining, role. The point of big poetry is to invoke an image of that kind of complex world. Post-modern theories of linguistics and economics have critiqued such views, and Nichols provides an excellent summary of the critiques and the counterarguments offered in Blaser's thought. "To summarize," she says, critiques of big poetry argue that

> poetry cannot take on the kind of big Dantean project Blaser proposes because first, there is no possibility of grasping the social whole on a planet where the global economy and private interests dictate policy and make a sham of democratic public engagement. Secondly, the stuff of experience – form and substance, self and other, the individual and society – has been superseded not only on the street but in philosophy (not to mention science), by processes that cannot be grasped as discrete. Hence there is no self to grasp a world that is not there anyway. Thirdly, the mediated nature of experience as it is shaped by various social determinants (language, the culture industry,

social place) and the cultural manyness of any conceivable
readership . . . undercuts the possibility of poetry as
idealization. (212)

Blaser counters these critiques, Nichols argues, with a redefinition
of public space and a revised understanding of experience within
that space. In "Particles" he proposes a space in which we share
our particularity, "our singular articulations of a sharable world"
(212-213). Blaser constructs an open-space poem wherein the
poet alongside other voices has agency to continually call out both
a world that could be and one that is. This is analogous, Nichols
argues, to Hannah Arendt's vision (in *The Human Condition*) of a
truly public arena as a "space of appearances" for differently situated
voices (213).

> What is proposed as an idealization is no one perspective
> and certainly not that of the poet, but rather the poem as
> meta-structure – as the space itself – that, through the
> accommodation of your view and mine, his view and hers,
> the living and the dead, offers measure and method, so we
> can see what everybody is doing and hence who we are.
> (214)

Nichols' crisp, well-organized discussion takes us to the
heart of Blaser's vision: poetry is a way of knowing. It is relational
thinking, not information, not facts. It is a performance of being in the
world that contains the soul and the divine and all the other human
things, all of which must be kept alive in memory. The poet does not
close the real into the individual ego; rather the poet's job is to make
the public world present, always remembering that the words are not
the poet's. Indeed, Blaser invoked a "wild logos": "there is no hard
boundary between language and the world, no point at which we
can separate words and things any more than we can reduce them
to each other. A *wild-logos* keeps the interchange between language
and experience moving" (154). The poet does not give us a stable
picture of the world; the poet gives us a distinctive performance of
being in the world which remains fluid, constantly shifting. Reality,
Blaser believed, "*is not a determinant entity. Reality is the great
unknown and unknowable.* We are constantly in quest of it, yet we

can never fully know it and certainly we cannot possess it: the best we can hope for is to preserve our capacity for encountering reality in some of its aspects" (he is quoting Louis Dudek (*The Fire* 272) (173).

Performing the real in relation to all the surrounding otherness is the poet's office.

A Crazy Angle, But Timeless:
From Nature
by Alan Bernheimer

Norman Fischer

I'm writing this in midst of our dramatic American moment — Black Lives Matter and the intense and unsettling conversation about race it's brought about; the distress of the Presidential election, as of now, six weeks on; wildfires in California and Oregon that make climate change seem to be an apocalyptic happening of the moment (while a record number of hurricanes siege the East coast); and of course the Covid-19 pandemic, that's stopped the whole world cold. (Maybe by the time you read this we are into fresh new crises, and all of the above seems distant).

It strikes me that in times like these, writers of all stripes, including poets, can't help but directly reflect what's going on in their works — didn't they/we all do this in the 9/11 moment twenty years ago? — or in the Vietnam era decades before that? —and how much more now, when the whole world seems to be collapsing around our ears. I myself, like so many of my friends, have written my own pandemic poem ("There Was a Clattering As..." to be published by Lavender Ink). But I wonder about this. What are writers — specifically poets — supposed to write in times of crisis (times are almost always in crisis)? Yeats famously wrote about the

Irish rebellion (but Joyce didn't). There are plenty of war novels and war poems (but how much of the poetry we want to read is about all that?). Holocaust poems, anti-slavery and anti-racism poems. Lefty novels and poems on the 1930's. So yes, there is that. But still the question in my mind is, is the poem obliged to reflect the times explicitly, as so many poems are doing now (to the point where it seems to be not ok to write about anything that isn't political)? Implicitly? (imagery or thematics that obliquely ie "poetically" express what's going on in the world outside the poem)? Or go beyond (or, some might say, irresponsibly avoid) what's happening to shape an aesthetic or moral message or non-message that affirms humanity, life, the goodness of the world (Ashbery?). What's poetry supposed to do here? All of the above, no doubt, but I'm not settled with the question, which is for me open, uncomfortable, and necessary to engage.

Now I'm reading *From Nature* by my friend Alan Bernheimer. The works that comprise this book (published in 2019 by Cunieform Press) were written much earlier, and of course do not reflect the moment in which I am writing this review (nor the moment in which you are reading it — and that's the problem too, isn't it, the moment passes so quickly, and what of it remains?). Yet I am reading the book now, in this moment, which conditions my reading of the poems as much as or maybe more than the moment in which they were written.

From Nature, and Alan's writing in general, doesn't directly reflect an historical moment. It's, in a way, art for its own sake, not pointing to a particular world outside the poem; a kind of eternal space that is essentially static. At the same time, the poems are not puffed up nor aesthetisized nor removed from the world; they're intensely colloquial, down to earth, telegraphic almost, like strung together series of surrealistic advertising aphorisms. Written from the perspective not of an historical moment but of an absolute present moment — in which the poet (anyone) is engaged with full concentration in the placing of words and phrases, sometimes sentences, stanzas, into poems. These poems are floating, flying, maybe falling through space (as Rae Armantrout notes in her blurb on the back cover) but not about to crash or even land anywhere.

Lots of jump cuts, sudden deft swerves, accomplished without fanfare, since there are only swerves, so there is nothing remarkable about them. The net effect of all this (to this reader at least) is to a sense of calm, a sense, oddly, of stability and sanity: this is, simply, reality in thought and word: it goes on with full confidence, never ending: it doesn't necessarily add up and yet it does: to lines, phrases, that come on loud and clear, one after another. What I'm saying here is that art's formality — and in this case the masterful formality and linguistic command that these poems effortlessly and modestly display — is comforting, and provides necessary relief from the catastrophes of the street (it's hard to remember when you read today's drastic news that there are happy and transcendent moments, even in a war zone) and a little light of hopefulness useful especially when hope seems in such short supply.

From Nature (the phrase doesn't appear in any of the poems; I take it to be a reference — in this case ironic— to paintings made "from nature") consists of three sections. The first, "Sleeping with Sirens", contains fifteen short poems of varying length; the second, "Beautilities", is a series of short dream-like prose poems (that read like recordings of actual dreams); the third, "The Spoonlight Institute", is a poem in 13 sections.

All three sections are strictly and carefully formal: the poems in the first section are written mostly in three line stanzas, with some in couplets (a couple are sonnets, 3X4+2). The second is in precise sentences. The third in couplets, 13 per poem (13 poems X 13 couplets per poem— bad luck?).

The imposition of such formality produces, as I say, a calming feeling: every hair's in place, no surprises, no shocks. A timeless feeling. Sheltering in place. Which, it seems, is what these poems are about: the timeless immediacy of language and thought (that remain intact in the background, even amidst historical tumult). The first line of the poem "The New Sentience" (a play on Ron Silliman's famous The New Sentence) is "It feels great being anyplace."

Here is the poem "Time out of Mind" from the first section. It's the one of only two poems in the book not in triplets or couplets, and consists of a series of questions about time that do not, strangely and significantly, end with questions marks:

What sorts of things are instants of time

Are events metaphysically basic

If we lived forever would there be a sense of time

Is time fossilized in the structure of language

Can time be completely empty

Are events pairs of a sentence that is true

Is the present made out of time

Can folks reject time theory without changing the topic

Is time our escape from contradiction

Can events recur or persist

Why is no sense assigned to time

Must participants exist when writing events occur

Are more assumptions than needed to get the job done ontologically extravagant

Is time a manifold of metaphorically basic points

Are we ideologically committed to the present being special or specious

And if you like your abstract speculations about time a little more concrete, there's this delightful prose poem from Beautilities:

"Ars Longa"

Marcel Duchamp, giving a talk, standing at a table on a loft floor in New York City. A man of eighty, he is as dapper and as fresh as a man of thirty, dark hair and an unlined face. Then I am introduced to his father, a man who appears to be in his late fifties.

    I'll conclude with another prose poem from this section that says or can be said to say in a few words what I've been arguing in this review:

"Liberty"

A sailboat cuts across a blue surface with a rectilinear grid of hemispherical depressions, the cusps between capped by white. In the background stands Liberty, mouth agape, dropping her book, torch tilted at a crazy angle.

Ladders of Light:
Mei-mei Berssenbrugge's
A Treatise on Stars

Hank Lazer

All around are invisible realities where contact may occur. (29)

My book describes how communicating with star beings can teach us to continue our world through love and grace, communal grace. (99)

I think I may be able to tell you exactly when I began reading Mei-mei Berssenbrugge's poetry with intense engagement and joy. For quite a few years when I'd encounter Berssenbrugge's poetry I skipped across its surface, like a stone skipping on a pond, somehow not quite slowing down enough, not placing my implicit expectations aside, to really read and absorb her poetry. It was December 2015, and I was taking part in the Rohatsu Sesshin at the Upaya Zen Center in Santa Fe, and Norman Fischer (poet and Zen priest), in a couple of dharma talks read portions of poems from Berssenbrugge's then newest book, *Hello, the Roses*. And it all clicked. Perhaps due to the ways in which seven days of meditation practice can clear, open, and slow down the mind?

I mention this experience because most reviews and essays have a pretense that the level of understanding being expressed was always that way, was somehow involved in a kind of steady-state permanence, which, of course, is absolutely not true. Reading, like writing, is unpredictable – in its intensity, engagement, in its surprises. Reading, like writing, changes over time.

I now understand Berssenbrugge's poetry, particularly *Treatise*, as a kind of instruction manual – phenomenological (refreshing how we see, hear, think), spiritual, strange, beautiful, other-worldly. It is an encouragement to us to become open to the vibrations of other beings and to the complexities of a quantum-physics world. From her own field notes – her experience of slowly attuning to other realities – we can learn how to move from the consensual hallucination we live within (i.e., an ego-centered Newtonian world and our habitual construct of "reality") to a much richer, more accurate, and more mystical multi-channel quantum world.

*

This is a stunning book.

Though the pronoun "I" appears throughout the book, these poems are not personal narratives in any traditional sense. Though many of the poems consist of observations and realizations, they take place *after* the self has dropped away. This particular sense of self will, as I develop more fully throughout this essay, is an essential aspect of what I mean by the Zen and Daoist nature of Berssenbrugge's *Treatise*.[1]

Comparing a star being to an angel reveals this context for constellations, extraterrestrials, conversations with animals.

You internalize space and ignite a photonic grid so bright as to be darkness to your untrained eyes.

___

[1] What I should make clear is that my own use of Zen and Daoist sources to inform and deepen my reading of *Treatise* is *not* meant to suggest that these are Berssenbrugge's sources. I would, though, claim that the consciousness that informs Mei-mei's writing has drawn upon and is very compatible with these perspectives.

When we enter into that closeness and unboundedness, it
feels like disintegration, like everywhere.

. . .

Where previously, vacuum meant empty; now it's invisible,
mobile energy; every point in space contains intersecting
light from every star. (67)

*

To develop and specify what I mean by the Zen and Daoist
elements in *Treatise*, Shunryu Suzuki's remarks on small mind / big
mind prove to be quite helpful. In *Not Always So: Practicing the
True Spirit of Zen*, Suzuki writes,

> To exist in big mind is an act of faith, which is different from
> the usual faith of believing in a particular idea or being. It is
> to believe that something is supporting us and supporting all
> our activities including thinking mind and emotional feelings.
> All these things are supported by something big that has
> no form or color. It is impossible to know what it is, but
> something exists there, something that is neither material
> nor spiritual. Something like that always exists, and we exist
> in that space. That is the feeling of pure being. (56)

In reading Berssenbrugge's *Treatise*, I feel like I am reading
about experiences that occur within an affirmation of big mind. Zen
thinking (if the term is not already oxymoronic) destabilizes any fixed
or common-sense notions of self and mind. As Suzuki suggests,

> We cannot find where the self is. … You think your mind is in
> your head, but where is it? No one knows. So our practice
> is to be with everything. Without being enslaved by it, you
> are able to share your practice with everything. That is how
> to establish yourself. You are ready to include everything.
> When you include everything, that is the real self. (*Not
> Always So*, 114).

In a similar vein, Lao Tzu's 7th poem of the *Tao Te Ching*

(translation by David Hinton) concludes,

> If you aren't free of yourself
> how will you ever become yourself?[2]

This self that one might become (through practice, through a forgetting of the small mind self) is hardly the self-expressive ego-centered self that typifies much of modern western poetry. The self of *Treatise* is one fully of its visible and invisible universe, a self of the same matter as that surrounding cosmos.

*

For some, Berssenbrugge's writing may not appear to be very "poetic," for it is written in long-lined sentences, and the sentence is the unit of composition. It is poetic, but without adornment. It is poetic in the depth and intensity of its wisdom. Plenty of great American poetry has been written in sentences – think of the work of Ron Silliman, or Lyn Hejinian, or Gertrude Stein. I find that Berssenbrugge's sentences/poems remind me most of the work of another visionary: William Blake. Berssenbrugge's *Treatise* sent me back to Blake's *The Marriage of Heaven and Hell*. While one of Blake's "A Memorable Fancy" sections concludes

> "How do you know but every bird
>
> that cuts the airy way
>
> Is an immense world of delight,
>
> closed by your senses five?"

which looks like "real" poetry, I find Berssenbrugge's work closer in spirit to the Proverbs of Hell section of Blake's work. The poetic passage just cited though conveys an aspect crucial to Berssenbrugge's *Treatise*. She is presenting a phenomenology

[2] I am grateful to Norman Fischer for reminding me that *Te* means virtue, as in the power of being what one truly is. Or, as David Hinton in the Key Terms to his translation of Lao Tzu's work notes, *Te*'s etymological meaning at the level of pictographic imagery is "heart-sight clarity."

of perception that seeks to question, understand, feel, and move beyond the limitations imposed by our life (often unexamined) lived within the parameters of our five senses. In Blake's Proverbs, several resonate with my reading experience of *Treatise*:

> The road of excess leads to the palace of wisdom.

> He whose face gives no light shall never become a star.

> What is now proved was once only imagined.

> Exuberance is Beauty.

Berssenbrugge's sentences are, unlike Blake's Proverbs, not pronouncements with the (seeming) finality of Blake's declarations: her sentences are more provisional, or pro-visionary, a prompt, a pointing toward the next sentence, as part of a series, a journey.

*

A typical phenomenological sequence in Berssenbrugge's book is not without feeling, not without emotion. But the emotion is rarely if ever located in a specific personal (small mind) domain. Rather, the emotion is simply part of an honest reporting:

> It's a mix of freedom and loneliness, and the loneliness is like space, so I look up at night sky.

> I see Sirius and try to communicate my emotions to a star, and information moves upward.

> Feeling utilizes a conscious grid connecting our sun with other stars, flowing along spiral nebulae; then Sirius becomes intrinsic, close, too bright to see all at once.

> All night, I feel subtle energy as stars reflect back the love I've given others.

> Photons flow into my eyes and transmute to my own cellular

structure.

> "Come out and stand with me;" you appear all at once, the
> way a window appears when I wake. (75)

Berssenbrugge's narrative phenomenology extends: "Later, thoughts
speed like shooting stars too fast to see, like starlight in other
frequencies of other heartbeats, to keep information flowing as we
feel chaotic, then change" (79). That is perhaps Berssenbrugge's
central preoccupation in *Treatise*: a study and experience of the
relationship between thinking and light.

*

Berssenbrugge observes: "Attention becomes thinking;
feeling divines a precise order of reality in imaginal space" (25),
and *Treatise* becomes a way to delineate an unfolding story of our
relatedness – to space, to stars, to light – by means of thinking:

> Your pulse aligns you with other light as a ladder of
> branches and leaves into heaven, with birds in the branches.
>
> Your focus is aliveness with another; we look with
> analogue, textile eyes at the dark field, generative gravity of
> consciousness. (27)

Berssenbrugge's experiential unfolding of this experience takes
her to the observation that "All life is this coherence of light being
emitted and received, then sometimes thought" (28).

*

When William Blake asked, " 'How do you know but every
bird/ that cuts the airy way/ Is an immense world of delight,/ closed
by your senses five?,' " he was far ahead of his time in considering
that each sentient species on earth was gifted with a different
sensory apparatus, and thus each species may be inhabiting a world
quite different than the one we assume to be *the real* according to
our five senses. Berssenbrugge observes, "Owls, for example, have

one song beyond the range of our hearing, interleaved with multi-dimensional information" (29). The world that we think is out there is a consequence of the aptitudes and limitations of our senses. That does not make it equal to the real. Berssenbrugge's *Treatise* is a speculative and experiential reaching into a more wondrous cosmos that we are part of, but that we do not readily access because it is closed to our five senses due to our unquestioned habits of perception.

*

Berssenbrugge's experience is sequential and points in the direction of light and thinking as shared:

> Brain steps down energy radiating from stars through optic nerve to pineal gland arranging these myriad photons into a neurological, space-time grid.

> It conveys the influx of light as a field, mentality.

> So thought is a form of organized light. (20)

Intensity of observation is the pathway to such realizations – and these are ultimately realizations of reciprocity and interactivity very much consistent with Daoist views of the cosmos, particularly as found in the *Tao Te Ching*. Berssenbrugge:

> A standing wave of photons comprises the immanent grid of starlight that permeates space; and vice versa, emanations from earth, sun, your nervousness and emotion radiate out.

> You observe this enigmatic dark energy, where every point in space contains intersecting photons from every star, past and present.

> Zero-sum, immense creativity streams through you, gyre of light as intelligence or your intent to observe. (21)

> Though it might make sense to say that Berssenbrugge's

thinking is *out there*, it is also clearly *in here*, as her *Treatise* interweaves our existence with that of the stars and the light in a mutually sustaining dance: "Nurture belief that your body's infused with the deep intelligence of this information, whose sole purpose is to sustain you" (21).

*

Berssenbrugge's notions of thinking and intelligence – arising from her experiences of the stars and starlight – strike me as akin to the non-dualistic relationship to thinking that is crucial to Zen practice. Norman Fischer, in *Training in Compassion: Zen Teachings on the Practice of Lojong* (a Tibetan system of mind-training), elaborates on the fifth slogan, "Rest in the openness of mind":

> The slogan **Rest in the openness of mind** describes a beautiful meditation practice and a beautiful feeling for life. It is a good description of Zen meditation practice, which I always think of as meditation beyond meditation. Not meditating on anything at all or trying to focus the mind or trying to calm the mind or do anything else. Zazen – Zen meditation – is, as one master [Dogen] says, "think not-thinking." It is resting in the openness of mind. Sometimes it's called not knowing. (22)

What Fischer and Dogen describe – and it is, I believe, central to Berssenbrugge's observations – is at once a deeply engaged thinking *and* a thinking that arrives at not-thinking. As Shohaku Okumura describes it in *The Mountains and Waters Sutra: A Practitioner's Guide to Dogen's "Sansuikyo,"*

> Dogen's method is to become free from our habitual way of thinking by thoroughly thinking. In Zen this is called "taking the wedge out by using the wedge." When we split wood we hit a wedge. Sometimes this wedge can neither come out nor go farther into the wood. So we use another wedge to widen the space; then we can remove the first wedge. Similarly, we use our thinking to liberate ourselves from our thinking. (184)

It is a process that allows one to be released from conceptual thinking. Or, as Suzuki describes it in his classic *Zen Mind, Beginner's Mind*,

> We say concentration, but to concentrate your mind on something is not the true purpose of Zen. The true purpose is to see things as they are, to observe things as they are, and to let everything go as it goes. … Zen practice is to open up our small mind. So concentrating is just an aid to help you realize "big mind," or the mind that is everything. (16).

*

What impresses me most about Berssenbrugge's *Treatise* is the interactivity and reciprocity of her vision. And vision is not the right word as the experiences she reports are, in the Buddhist conception, felt in all six senses (the sixth being mind). She writes from within a felt commonality, of self and cosmos as not two but one entity: "Our desire for light, for consciousness, is pulled from the transcendent domain of potential by the seeds of environment herself" (30). While her experience can be understood as engaged with a large frame ecopoetics, a reverence for the earth and the cosmos, she indicates, "I struggle for understanding beyond environmental fears and grief" (32). And that "beyond" I suggest comes from a radically intensive experience of consciousness: "I describe consciousness as mother, earth, and the intelligence that shapes it" (32). Very much in keeping with the Tibetan Buddhist slogan: "Rest in the openness of mind."

And thus we are beginning to locate Berssenbrugge's thinking within a sphere of thinking that includes William Blake, Lao Tzu, Tibetan Buddhism, Dogen, Norman Fischer, and others. When Berssenbrugge writes, "Later, I'm told the cosmos communicates with itself through this web of images we imagine" (37), her field of thinking merges with ancient Chinese perspectives on self and cosmos.

*

In writing about Dogen, Okumura offers a story of our place and purpose within the universe (as we share in the process of appearance and creation):

> Planet Earth is a tiny product of the evolution of this universe. We human beings are a tiny and relatively new part of nature on this small planet. And yet somehow we have an ability to observe the planet, the solar system, other galaxies, and even the entire universe, and we try to understand what they are, what is really happening, what is the origin of this movement of the universe. We even think about the meaning of all this movement. This is our attempt to see reality, to understand the meaning of our lives and this world. But we can look from another direction and say that because we are a part of the universe, the entire world is using human beings to see itself. In this sense the entire universe is studying itself through us. (104)

Okumura concludes (provisionally), "I think that is the basic premise of Dogen's teaching. The world creates me and I create the world. The mutual work is our life and our purpose" (75). From his beautifully nuanced reading of Dogen's "Sansuikyo," one of the most important texts produced by the 13th century founder of the Soto school of Zen Buddhism, Okumura arrives at a conclusion very much in keeping with the vision and experiences found in Berssenbrugge's *Treatise*:

> The world of sentient beings is everywhere, and the reality of all beings pervades every part of the universe. Each element of the universe and the universe as a whole permeate each other. This is the world of sentient beings for us sentient beings. (219)

Perhaps Dogen's thinking, and Berssenbrugge's as well, takes root in early Daoist and Zen perspectives. David Hinton, in several books and in his many translations from Chinese poetry, has done a superb job of articulating that world view, as in Berssenbrugge's *Treatise* articulating a non-dualistic participatory vision of our role from *within* and *of* that universe. In his introduction to *Awakened Cosmos: The Mind of Classical Chinese Poetry*, Hinton begins in a manner close to Suzuki's thinking about small mind / big mind:

> Poetry is the Cosmos awakened to itself. Narrative, reportage, explanation, idea: language is the medium of self-identity, and we normally live within that clutch of identity. Identity that seems to look out at and think about the Cosmos as if from some outside space. But poetry pares language down to a bare minimum, thereby opening it to silence. And it is there in the margins of silence that poetry finds its deepest possibilities – for there it can render dimensions of consciousness that are much more expansive than that identity-center, primal dimensions of consciousness as the Cosmos awakened to itself. At least this is true for classical Chinese poetry, shaped as it is by Taoist and Ch'an (Zen) Buddhist thought into a form of spiritual practice. In its deepest possibilities, its inner wilds, poetry is the Cosmos awakened to itself – and the history of that awakening begins where the Cosmos begins. (ix)

In Berssenbrugge's *Treatise*, with its long packed sentences, openings to silence occur in the white space between sentences and the space between sections of individual poems.

As Hinton extends this story of cosmic beginnings, he arrives at a point that might well serve as a fit introduction to Berssenbrugge's *Treatise*:

> Eventually, hydrogen and helium began condensing into proto-galactic clouds under the gossamer influence of gravity, and chance fluctuations in the density of these clouds led some local areas to intensify their condensation until pressure and heat became so fierce that hydrogen atoms began fusing together. In that process, which can only be described as magical, stars were born. And with those stars came the elemental dimensions of consciousness: space and light and the visible. (x)

Hinton concludes, "It is the heartbeat of the Cosmos, this steady pulse of stellar birth and death" (x). Berssenbrugge's *Treatise* pulsates with that heartbeat and is a location for stellar light to become thought.

*

Berssenbrugge's *Treatise* constitutes a cosmology, in the same way that pre-Socratics like Parmenides and Heraclitus could write a sentence and fragment-based poetry of what Suzuki would call big mind. Or, with the scope of Lucretius' *On the Nature of Things*. Berssenbrugge's is a cosmology experienced when the duality of subject and object has vanished in favor of a heuristic, bold, pedagogical (learning and instructing) interactivity:

> So, matter on earth was made in stars and scattered through space by star explosions.
>
> So, all particles in the universe are entangled.
>
> This state persists until measured by a conscious imagination as experience. (40)

Berssenbrugge's cosmology is a contemporary Daoist experience of interconnectedness – of all matter. It is an ongoing experiencing of conscious imagination as a portal for feeling and exploring that interconnectedness:

> Star-human communication occurs in mind first, then a way is prepared for contact.
>
> She tells them her hopes, which they amplify; beings align with her thought through an inner connection to their common source.
>
> ...
>
> You could say imagining has the point-like characteristic of creation. (41)

These lines begin to point toward one of the more audacious strands in *Treatise*: a communication that goes well beyond earth and earthlings. It is what in a sci fi context we would call contact with extraterrestrial beings. As we will see in later passages in *Treatise*, Berssenbrugge appears to be taking instruction and becoming a kind of initiate into these starry modes of correspondence and communication. Various lines sound like the testimony of others who have had the kinds of experiences that Berssenbrugge herself is now beginning to have. At the heart of these experiences – and of great pertinence to the nature of poetry itself – is a deepening understanding of thinking and imagining, and the sources for these experiences:

> Whether we come from the stars or from earth, we call stars "ancestors" out of respect.
>
> We connect by their light entering our eyes, and through our bodies we transcribe them. (44)

Similarly, Shunryu Suzuki suggests that "when we practice zazen, we are practicing with all the ancestors" (36, *Not Always So*).[3]

I experience *Treatise* as a kind of celestial instruction manual, a phenomenological account of Berssenbrugge's own experiences. She writes, "It's as if a star offered you the nourishing, ineffable light of a new realism between subject and object" (60). Indeed, *Treatise* throughout is a book written from *within* the experience of big mind. It is a book about thinking – where it comes from, its absolute and invisible (though tangible) nature and interconnectedness with all matter (especially light). But it is an about-ness written from *within* the experience itself. Berssenbrugge, again and again in *Treatise*, shows us experiencing intereconnectedness as generative, as an intensification of awareness, as a portal for insight and en-light-enment.

*

---

[3] 5/14/2020 – email from Mei-mei in response to my question about whether or not she had a developed meditation practice: "I always want to meditate, but speeding in my head, driven. Our nurse meditates and maybe we should do that together."

An aspect of Berssenbrugge's *A Treatise On Stars* that is so obvious that I have failed to mention it reveals itself as soon as we pay careful attention to the implications of the word *treatise*. That key word in the title immediately places her book (which is classified on the book cover as "poetry") also within the domain of science. (I also would suggest that Berssenbrugge's earlier book, *Hello, the Roses* [2013], with its acute attention to the nature of time, also is a kind of poetry quite at home in the sphere of scientific thinking.) The word *treatise* asks us to rethink what constitutes *poetry*. What intrigues me about this word is that it locates her book within a long history of poetic (meaning imaginative, far-reaching, adventurous, heuristic) scientific writing and thinking (which has, in the more distant past, often been written as poetry). It's a noble lineage that would include, among others, Democritus, Zeno, Pythagoras, Euclid, Ptolemy, Lucretius, Dante, Galileo, Newton, Bohr, Heisenberg, and Einstein.

In my own reading of late, I would suggest that it is the contemporary thinking in quantum physics that once again makes the path between poetry and science an open thoroughfare. To pick one wonderful recent book – Carlo Rovelli's *Reality Is Not What It Seems* (New York: Riverhead Books, 2017) – to illuminate these connections, we find Rovelli stating:

> Science is continual exploration of ways of thinking. Its strength is its visionary capacity to demolish preconceived ideas, to reveal new regions of reality, and to construct new and more effective images of the world. ... The world is boundless and iridescent; we want to go and see it. (8)

The discoveries in quantum physics places the human perceiver and the nature of reality within an interactive and relational framework very much at the heart of Berssenbrugge's own interactions with stars, light, and sounds.[4] Rovelli explains,

[4] 5/12/2020 – email from Mei-mei regarding source-reading for *Treatise* – "By the time I started Stars, I was weary of straight science or philosophy books, and interested in cosmological/spiritual combinations. Here are some I read, that including a couple of buddhist titles. I also read a lot of native american and south american astronomy and oral accounts and Extra terrestrial oral accounts." Mei-mei provided me with a long list of the books (26 books!) she had been reading while writing *Treatise*; indeed, some of her readings are more in the direction of "cosmology" rather than "pure science," while

The third discovery about the world articulated by quantum mechanics is the most profound and difficult – and one that was not anticipated by the atomism of antiquity. The theory does not describe things as they "are": it describes how things "occur," and how they "interact with each other." It doesn't describe *where* there is a particle but how the particle *shows itself to others*. The world of existent things is reduced to a realm of possible interactions. Reality is reduced to interaction. Reality is reduced to relation. In a certain sense, this is just an extension of relativity, albeit a radical one. (134-135)

Rovelli concludes,

I believe that in order to understand reality, we have to keep in mind that reality is this network of relations, of reciprocal information, that weaves the world. We slice up the reality surrounding us into "objects." But reality is not made up of discrete objects. It is a variable flux. (254)

Rovelli's description of adaptive organisms strikes me as very much in keeping with the protean, interactive perceptual experiences that are central to the adventuring of Berssenbrugge's *Treatise*: "A living organism is a system that continually re-forms itself in order to remain itself, interacting ceaselessly with the external world" (255).

*

The interconnectedness at the heart of Berssenbrugge's experiences in *Treatise* reminds me of Suzuki's conclusion that "We ourselves cannot put any magic spells on this world. The world is its own magic" (46, *Zen Mind*).

Okumura's *The Mountains and Waters Sutra: A Practitioner's Guide to Dogen's "Sansuikyo"* includes as an appendix some writing by Gary Snyder, including Snyder's remarks at a 1999 symposium on "Dogen Zen and Its Relevance for Our Time." I cite Snyder's

---

also exploring connections between cosmology, astronomy, physics, and Zen perspectives.

remarks (from twenty-one years ago!) to demonstrate the ecological and ethical perspectives implicit throughout Berssenbrugge's *Treatise*:

> But scientific information in itself does not move governments, world leaders, or masses of people. To transform public policy in regard to the oceans and air, forests, and population questions, and to move toward saving endangered species, both require reaching the very hearts of whole societies. This is not a work for the scientists. Their research is essential to us, but to change the way contemporary human beings live on earth is a kind of Dharma work, a work for dedicated followers of the Way who because of their practice and insight can hope to balance wisdom and compassion and help open the eyes of others. I think that Buddhism, and especially old Shamon Dogen, has something to show us in the matter of how to go about this. (241)

At the heart of Dogen's thinking, and Snyder's, and Berssenbrugge's, is an overcoming of the self-centeredness of the human species:

> We of the cusp of the third millennium of Late Capitalism, might also identify with the best-known facet of Dogen, that is, Dogen as a teacher who helps us skillfully grasp the truth that all realms are authentic and then teaches how to overcome human-species ego, as well as personal ego. (243)

As Snyder noted in 1999, remarks unfortunately even more true in the US of 2020, "...I am speaking as a person from a backward society that is equally far from the land of the Buddha and the Land of Plato – inhabited by self-righteously ignorant people, some of whom don't even want to hear about Darwinian evolution, let alone the Dharma" (243).

*

While some of the comparisons and kinships I've suggested might seem oddly wide-ranging and arbitrary, what prompts these linkages is an audacity, vision, and clarity in Berssenbrugge's *Treatise*. The sheer audacity of *Treatise* reminds me of the performative mysticism of poets/artists Hannah Weiner, Linda Montano, and Cecilia Vicuña. I am linking Berssenbrugge's work to other visionary works of the first order; these artists offer rituals steeped in immediacy.

I wish to slow down to provide a more extended sense of what I mean by the performative element in Berssenbrugge's *Treatise*, doing so by means of the poem "Singing," which begins, "All day, I feel the approach of dolphins, their thoughts are in my mind./ When I swim, my cells attune to them, because ocean's full of vibrations that transmit to water in my body" (81). Though much of her *Treatise* depends upon an attunement to light and the transmissions and vibrations through light as a corresponding fuel for thinking, "Singing" (I present section 2 of this poem) gives us a sequential understanding (or experiencing) by means of hearing-as-transmission:

I empty my mind and listen for her reply, which comes as waves of emotion.

A cloud surrounds me; I expand into its stillness and receive tones conveying information very fast.

They teach me to hum, to whistle and sing; sound amplifies my body across open water; even their joyous play has this sensation of creating space, and when they sleep, stars augment their frequencies.

We converse by mind-cell helixes of image and feeling.

Cosmic legacy, cosmic extension imprint holographically on my heart neurons as dolphin empathy.

There are sounds which can stop time, alter surroundings or shift your dimension.

Swimming I lose my sense of place, even physicality and
connect with collective love.

They teach me to join my aura with the cosmos by spiraling
with me in sound-star tetrahedrons and to love those with
whom we merge.

Then being is healing, through innocence, when the animal
becomes the teacher. (82)

In a later poem in *Treatise*, "New Boys 2," Berssenbrugge
writes about one of her informants or conversational partners, "More
often now, ETs are discussed at the co-op, also coincidence, spirit
molecules, time tunnels and quantum uncertainty, since we're close
to the Santa Fe Institute./ I like that he expresses himself to me
as a kind of witness in transition" (88). She too presents herself
to us as "a kind of witness in transition," one who skirts the edges
of a trendy shallow New Age-ism, who instead presents us with a
profound depth of phenomenological understanding and years of
practice preparing her poems and her experiences to plumb (and
report) these depths.

*

As the ego or small mind dissolves, the poet is able to
receive fully, to be possessed, to become a medium, though all of
these descriptions are in some sense too dramatic and too amped
up. In *Treatise*, we find that "Many intelligences reveal themselves
through animals or plants. / Ask for a grand enhancement of your
identity through trust, through living in the moment, as you sit at your
desk" (93). When I say "possession" I think of it as a meditative
experience, an emptiness that allows for receptivity: "One part
of myself is taking dictation, while one part enjoys a calm, empty
day" (93). It is an emptiness that sends as well as receives: "You
too radiate light to other worlds seeking to know their creation"
(95). Berssenbrugge becomes a scribe, as in Daoist cosmology:
an intelligence that is of the same matter as the cosmos and with
the ability to reflect back to the cosmos its own nature by means of
writing (and consciousness and shared light). So that "When I see

stunning photographs of earth from space, she has the organized, self-contained look of a living being" (95). All that is alive is our teacher: "Those formerly referred to as animals love unconditionally, mentoring us" (96).

If there is humor (and there is, and also joy) at the heart of Berssenbrugge's *Treatise*, it rests in the sense that a poet often has with a completed book:

Early on, I divined that this book already exists in the future.

After all, I thought of it; it's a probability somewhere, complete on a shelf.

My intention is to consult that future edition and create this one, the original, for you. (91)

We see and feel and sense the book that we are, and the book that we are writing toward. Having already felt and foreknown its existence, we ride it out, and we write it out… Then, others can read it, ride it, radiate out, learning how by means of this gift, the *Treatise*.

Joe Porter's Artistry

Toby Olson

I first met Joe Porter in the early 1990s when he was writer-in-residence at Brown University. I was there with my wife Miriam looking for a job that never materialized. We had dinner together, and Miriam remarked that Joe's book *Eelgrass* was her favorite novel. Joe was pleased to hear this, and the two leaned toward each other and spoke intimately about their lives and his writing. Joe was a gentleman, kind and attentive, much like those characters that people many of his books.

While *Eelgrass* appeared a good while ago, the relaxed and charming way that novel works as a lightly comic analogue to Shakespear's "The Tempest" suggests, given my reading of the concluding story in *All Aboard*, that "Forgotten Coast," Joe's last (I believe as yet unpublished) novel follows in that line. And the way in which his novel *Resident Aliens,* as well as many of his short stories, edges into the autobiographical, points to this final work as a reasonable extension of ongoing concerns.

The story of "Forgotten Coast" is a conventional one, a family saga set mostly in the Florida beach side town of Apalachicola, but this conventional story, replete with a gathering of odd characters, is delivered through an innovative prose that seems to me unique. The narrator here intrudes in the doings in a way that makes him (or her) seems a character in his own right. At once objective and comic, sadly ironic and burlesque, I'm reminded of Jose Saramago's way in the novel *Blindness*, though Porter's writing manner is all his own, and if it nods to anyone, it nods to Shakespear, the author that Porter had studied and written about in many scholarly essays.

Joe Ashby Porter wrote a significantly large body of work that covers a broad spectrum of tones and manners, everything from parody and the strangely comic to the darkly romantic and political. Many of his fictions stand as models against which the contemporary American short story might be measured, and his three published novels only extend his skills to the longer form. He was as powerful there as he was with the story.

"Forgotten Coast" represents a fitting end to a career cut sadly short, leaving us with a perfect example of Joe Ashby Porter's mastery.

Notes on Contributors

Rae Armantrout is the author of fifteen books of poems, including *Conjure* (Wesleyan, 2020), *Wobble* (2018), a finalist for the National Book Award, *Partly, New and Selected Poems* (2016), and *Versed* (2009) which won the Pulitzer Prize and the National Book Critics Circle Award in 2010. An "Art of Poetry" interview with Armantrout, conducted by Brian Reed, was published in *The Paris Review* in Dec., 2019. She is professor emerita at UC San Diego and currently lives in Washington State.

Ian Brinton's most recent publications include *Islands of Voices*, selected poems of Douglas Oliver (Shearsman Books). His translation of Paul Valéry's selected poems, with a Preface by Michael Heller, will appear from Muscaliet Press in early 2021 and *Paris Scenes*, a translation of Baudelaire's 'Tableaux Parisiens' will appear in July from Two Rivers Press.

Joel Chace has published work in print and electronic magazines such as *The Tip of the Knife, Unlikely Stories, Eratio, Otoliths, Word For/Word,* and *Jacket.* Most recent collections include *Kansoz*, from Knives, Forks, and Spoons Press, *War, and After*, from BlazeVOX,

Scorpions, from Unlikely Books, *Humors*, from Paloma Press, and *Threnodies*, from Moria Books.

Joseph Donahue's most recent volumes of poetry are *Wind Maps I-VII* (Talisman 2018), and *The Disappearance of Fate* (Spuyten Duyvil, 2019). He is the co-translator of *First Mountain* (Zephyr Press, 2018), by Zhang Er. Two volumes of his ongoing poetic sequence, *Terra Lucida*, are forthcoming from Verge Books.

Rachel Blau DuPlessis is the author of the multivolume long poem *Drafts* (written between 1986 and 2012), the recent collage poems *NUMBERS* (2018) and *Graphic Novella* (2015), Her second long poem, now in process called *Traces, with Days*, includes *Days and Works* (Ahsahta, 2017); *Late Work* (Black Square Editions, 2020); *Around the Day in 80 Worlds* (BlazeVOX, 2018), and *Poetic Realism* (BlazeVOX, forthcoming 2021). Her *Selected Poems 1980-2020* will come out from CHAX in 2022. A *Collected Drafts* is planned by Black Square Editions. She is also writing a critical book provisionally titled *A Long Essay on the Long Poem*.

Forough Farrokhzad (1934-1967) was the most important female Iranian poet of the 20th century. She broke all the rules. This daughter of a military officer married a cousin at sixteen, gave birth to her son, Kamyar, at seventeen, was divorced at nineteen and, deprived of her son, moved to Tehran to begin a solo career as a poet and documentary filmmaker. She studied abroad, lived openly with the filmmaker Ebrahim Golestan, and published poems that spoke openly and frankly about love, sex, loneliness, and devastating loss, from a feminine point of view. Her short film about a leper colony in northwestern Iran, *The House Is Black*, won international awards and broke ground for Iran's New Cinema. Farrokhzad was killed in an automobile accident at the age of 32.

Norman Fischer is a poet, essayist, and Zen Buddhist priest. The latest of his more than thirty prose and poetry titles are the serial poems *Untitled Series: Life As It Is* (Talisman House) and *On a Train At Night* (Presse Universite de Rouen et Havre). Forthcoming from Tuumba is *Nature* (of which the piece here in an excerpt). Forthcoming from Lavender Ink is his *There Was a Clattering As….*" a pandemic poem. Forthcoming from Shambhala Press is a collection of his Buddhist essays, *When You Greet Me I Bow.* He is the founder of the Everyday Zen Foundation (www.everydayzen.org), a network of Zen meditation groups and other projects. His books are at www.NormanFischer.org.

Nancy Gaffield is the author of six poetry publications, including *Meridian* (Longbarrow Press 2019), *Continental Drift* (Shearsman 2014), and *Tokaido Road* (CB editions 2011). She adapted *Tokaido Road* into a libretto; the opera, composed by Nicola LeFanu, premiered at the Cheltenham Music Festival in 2014 before touring the UK in 2015. She has also published three chapbooks, including most recently *Wealden*, which explores the consonance between nature, poetry and electronic music (www.longbarrwpress.com). She is an honorary academic in Creative Writing at the University of Kent.

Jesse Glass. After a run of nineteen years at Meikai University, Jesse Glass is now gainfully retired as Professor Emeritus in the wilds of Tokyo. Recent work featured in *The Fortnightly Review, Gargoyle* and a new selected sequences out next year from The Knives Forks and Spoons Press. Ekleksographia/ Ahadada Books is back with a new Ahadada Reader in the works.

Danielle Hooke Goodbody is from Chicago, but has lived in the UK since 2009. She is currently a PhD student at the University of Kent, Canterbury. Recent work appears in *Tenebrae II* and *Lighthouse*.

Elizabeth T. Gray, Jr. is a poet, translator, and corporate consultant. Her long poem, *Salient*, was published by New Directions in May 2020. Other recent publications include the poetic sequence *Series I India* (Four Way Books, 2015) and translations from classical Persian, *Wine & Prayer: Eighty Ghazals of Hafiz of Shiraz* (White Cloud Press, 2019). *Selected Poems of Forough Farrokhzad*, translations of Iran's most important modern woman poet, is forthcoming from New Directions in 2022. She has served as Guest Editor for *Epiphany* and *The New Haven Review* and currently serves on the Boards of Friends of Writers, *The Beloit Poetry Journal* Foundation, and of Human Rights and Democracy in Iran. She holds a BA and JD from Harvard University and an MFA from Warren Wilson College.

www.elizabethtgrayjr.com

Peter Hughes was born in Oxford, UK. His mother is Irish and his father's forebears came from north Wales. Peter is a poet and the founding editor of Oystercatcher Press. He has been Visiting Fellow in Poetry at Cambridge University and is currently based on the northern margins of Snowdonia. He lived for several years in Italy and has created innovative versions of poems by Petrarch and Cavalcanti. His most recent book is *A Berlin Entrainment* (Shearsman, 2019).

Trevor Joyce co-founded New Writers' Press in Dublin in 1967, and SoundEye in Cork in 1997. He held the Judith E Wilson Fellowship for poetry to the University of Cambridge for 2009/10, and in 2017 was awarded the biennial N. C. Kaser prize for poetry. His recent books include *The Immediate Future* (2013), *Rome's Wreck* (2014), *Selected Poems* (2014), and *Fastness* (2017). He is a member of Aosdána.

Hank Lazer has published thirty-two books of poetry, including *COVID19 SUTRAS* (2020, Lavender Ink), *Slowly Becoming Awake* (N32) (2019, Dos Madres Press), and *Poems That Look Just Like Poems* (2019, PURH – one volume in English, one in French), In 2015, Lazer received Alabama's most prestigious literary prize, the Harper Lee Award, for lifetime achievement in literature. Lazer has been quarantining in Tuscaloosa, Alabama, and at Duncan Farm in Carrollton, Alabama.

Dorothy Lehane is the author of four poetry publications: *Bettbehandlung* (Muscaliet Press, 2018), *Umwelt* (Leafe Press, 2016), *Ephemeris* (Nine Arches Press, 2014), and *Places of Articulation* (dancing girl press 2014). She has read her work to audiences at Université Sorbonne, Ivy Writers, Paris, the Science Museum, the Wellcome Trust, the Barbican, the Roundhouse, BBC Radio Kent, and the Union Chapel, and has contributed on improvised collaborations, notably with synthesizer Matthew Bourne. Recent poetry and reviews appear in *Westerly Magazine, Glasfryn Project* and *Modern Philology.* She teaches Creative Writing at the University of Kent and is currently writing a memoir on the lived autoimmune experience, titled: *Reactive: a memoir of an unknowable body.*
The poetic sequence *House-girl* is interested in how the fear

of contagion is inscribed into disease and has historically provoked hysteria, revulsion, and an enduring tradition of stigmatisation. In this excerpt, siblings perform ceremonies using potions and medicines from the natural world, carrying out diagnosis and treatments for disease.

Since the late 1960's **Peter de Lory** has been working professionally as a photographer. A major portion of his work has focused on issues in the American West, particularly the evolving relationships between human and landscape. The evolution of his work and interests mirror the landscapes and structures around him. He photographs in a very formal straightforward way structurally, freeing the subject up for interpretation, creating an opening for emotion and meaning in the work. He is represented in Seattle by the Harris Harvey Gallery, and has works in numerous national and region collections.

Nathaniel Mackey's most recent book of poetry is *Blue Fasa* (New Directions, 2015). Forthcoming from New Directions in 2021 is *Double Trio*, a three-book set.

Andrew Mossin has published six books of poetry, most recently *The Fire Cycle* (Spuyten Duyvil) and a collection of critical essays, *Male Subjectivity and Poetic Form in "New American" Poetry* (Palgrave). He has recently completed a book-length memoir, *A Son From the Mountains: A Story of Adoption, Family Separation and Violence*, and is at work on a new book of poetry, tentatively titled *The Common World*. He is an Associate Professor in the Intellectual Heritage Program at Temple University in Philadelphia.

John Muckle lives in London and works as a teacher. In the eighties he initiated the Paladin poetry imprint, and was general editor of its flagship anthology, *The New British Poetry*. He has published fiction, poetry and criticism, including *Cyclomotors, London Brakes, My Pale Tulip, Little White Bull: British Fiction in the 50s and 60s*, and his most recent poetry collection, *Mirrorball*. His new stories are from a just published book, *Late Driver* (Shearsman, 2020).

Toby Olson's most recent works include the novel *Walking* (Occidental Square Books) and a gathering of poems, *Death*

Sentences (Shearsman). "Journeys On A Dime," his selected short stories, will appear from Grand Iota in the coming year.

Meredith Quartermain has just launched her fourth book of poems: *Lullabies in the Real World*, a playful interrogation of colonial and literary history. *Vancouver Walking* won a BC Book Award for Poetry, and *Nightmarker* was a finalist for a Vancouver Book Award. Other books include *Recipes from the Red Planet* (finalist for a BC Book Award in fiction); *I, Bartleby: short stories*; and *U Girl: a novel*. From 2014 to 2016, she was Poetry Mentor in the SFU Writer's Studio Program, and in 2012 she was Vancouver Public Library Writer in Residence.

Peter Quartermain is the author of two books of critical essays: *Stubborn Poetries* and *Disjunctive Poetics*. He edited the award winning two-volume *Collected Poems and Plays* of Robert Duncan, and co-edited two other collections. He has now completed his memoir of wartime England, *Growing Dumb: My English Education*, and is looking for a publisher. "Robin and Jim" is an excerpt from that memoir.

Eléna Rivera was born in Mexico City and raised in Paris, France. Her most recent book is *Epic Series* from Shearsman Books (2020). Her book *Scaffolding* (2017) is available from Princeton University Press. She received a National Endowment for the Arts and Literature Fellowship in Translation and was a recent recipient of fellowships from the Trelex Paris Poetry Residency (2019) and the SHOEN Foundation (2016).

Maurice Scully's most recent books are *Play Book* (Coracle Press, 2019) & *Things That Happen* (Shearsman 2020). The poems here are from a new book in process, *Airs*.

Zoë Skoulding lives on Anglesey and is Professor of Poetry and Creative Writing at Bangor University. Recent poetry collections include *Footnotes to Water* (Seren, 2019), which won the Wales Book of the Year Poetry Award 2020; *The Celestial Set-Up* (Oystercatcher, 2020) and *A Revolutionary Calendar* (Shearsman, 2020). Her critical work includes *Poetry & Listening: The Noise of Lyric* (Liverpool

University Press, 2020). She received the Cholmondeley Award from the Society of Authors in 2018 for her body of work in poetry.

♋♌♍♎♏♐♑♒♓☊☋●○■□□

www.ingramcontent.com/pod-product-compliance
Lightning Source LLC
Chambersburg PA
CBHW072229170626
46813CB00003B/1143